ETERNITY FOR SALE

"Time, the avenger! Unto thee I lift,
My hands and eyes, and heart, and crave of thee a gift."

- Lord Byron

Renate Yates

For My Family.

Published by

Unit 2, 2-4 Notts Avenue
Bondi Beach, NSW 2026
AUSTRALIA

trilby@svengalipress.com.au
www.svengalipress.com.au

ISBN 978-0-6489227-2-8
Copyright © 2021 Renate Yates

ISBN 978-1-922473-82-0 (ebook)
Published in association with ETT Imprint, Exile Bay

CONTENTS

CHAPTER ONE

Mrs. Jenkins, the cleaning lady from the village, wearing the traditional cigarette dependant from her lower lip swished her feather duster over the Louis Quinze clock on the mantelpiece with a flourish, the flourish having rather more elan than any potential for dust removal. Next she swirled the feathers over the clock on the marble plinth by the window, wondering, not for the first time why Sir Basil needed to surround himself with so many clocks.

'Ostentatious that's what it is, not to mention noisy,' she muttered, passing the duster over the face of the large grandfather clock standing in the alcove, its pendulum swinging with a heavy and ominous ponderousness. In Mrs. Jenkins world people who collected artifacts of any kind (and that included stamps, coins and match boxes) were halfway around the bend. She was a practical woman who threw things out. Not for her the continuity of possessions.

'I'm off then- my time's well and truly up' she told the small carriage clock on the side table and flung the remains of her cigarette through the French window out into the garden. She packed up her things and went into the hall where she deftly hurled her feather duster into the cupboard under the stairs. She returned to the drawing room for her handbag just as the doorbell rang. No one came to answer it and Mrs. Jenkins sighed loudly. The bell rang again.

'Who do they think I am, the butler?' she asked the grandfather clock and grumpily opened the front door. A tall, well-built man stood on the threshold, beside him masses of luggage- a number of suitcases as well as a tripod and camera and projection equipment.

'Come in,' said Mrs. Jenkins 'and put that stuff down anywhere. I'm sure I don't know where she's got to – should have been here to pay me- I'm a busy person you know- only come up here to do her a favour- got a family of me own to look after. Big week-end coming up too- her birthday and all...' Mrs. Jenkins drew breath and hit her forehead with the flat of her hand '...silly me...now I remember where she's gone- to get her birthday cake. Mrs. Payne in the village makes a lovely cake, rich fruit and icing that thick.' She indicated the magnanimous extent of the icing with her thumb and forefinger.

The stranger, having put down his equipment in the hall during this monologue appeared surprised.

'I didn't know it was her birthday- what a shame, if I'd known I would have brought a gift.' Mrs. Jenkins too registered surprise.

1

'I say- you're from America,' she told him. 'That's correct- I'm from California.' Mrs. Jenkins looked at him warily. 'Dangerous place America- if we're to believe everything we see on the telly.' Mrs. Jenkins believed implicitly in television power.

'America,' she repeated 'too many guns, that's what I say.' The American nodded his agreement.

'Well' she continued 'I'll be off then. Tell her I'll be in on Monday- barring accidents that is.' She smiled at her little joke and banged the front door behind her.

Dr. Charles Huxley, marveling at Mrs. Jenkins trusting nature despite her suspicions of Americans in general, moved into the drawing room. He could hardly believe his luck. To meet an authentic piece (if Mrs. Jenkins could be described as a piece) of olde England, a 'character' as preserved on film and television, almost immediately upon arrival in this strange land was a good omen. His visit would be a success he felt for sure of it. Every optimistic fibre of his U.S.A. (West Coast) soul vibrated with confidence.

He found himself in a large room dominated by a spacious fireplace. On tables stood photographs in silver frames. On the walls hung gloomy portraits (presumably of ancestors) in gilded frames. Of clocks there were an abundance. Three French windows gave onto a garden. In the distance, beyond a series of impeccably clipped hedges he saw a beautiful and, even from this distance, obviously slightly decrepit, though massive, Queen Ann house. At that moment a figure appeared at one of the French doors, wrenched it open and in its hurry almost fell into the room. Charles saw a very old lady dressed improbably but certainly recognisably, as Mae West. Her make-up was heavy and luridly colourful. The slightly moth-eaten feathers in her huge pink hat flew and fluttered as she advanced upon Charles. 'Aren't I clever,' she whispered conspiratorially, 'I've given him the slip.' A bemused Charles asked, 'Who-given who the slip?' 'Steve, my jailer. He simply will not leave me alone- always nagging- do this, don't do that, I'm terribly tired of him- it's so incredibly tedious don't you know. I mean a girl has a right to be alone every now and again don't you think so?' Her accent, as much as Charles could judge seemed to him flawlessly English. He held out his hand, 'How do you do- I guess you must be Lady Clarissa Hare Bell....'

'Don't be silly young man I'm not Clarissa- you must have recognised me,' she posed seductively, a hand to her crimson cheek, 'I'm Mae West, the famous or infamous,' she giggled like a girl 'Mae West. I was born in 1893 in Tennessee, the Deep South you know- but of course you can hear that from my accent. I...' she paused dramatically and threw out her beringed hands as to an entranced audience, '…I will live forever.' Charles Huxley closed his mouth which had involuntarily opened and had remained open during this speech and stammered, 'I…I…guess you will at that.'

'There's no guessing about it young man, I will, I certainly will live forever. Everyone knows me- I'm the bad girl of Broadway. I used to be the Snow White but I drifted.' She waited for laughs from her captive audience. Charles Huxley quite lost smiled weakly and guessed again, 'I guess it must be your daughter I've come to see…' Mae West frowned, 'I have no children- you ought to know that, never had the time. In any case having babies is extremely bad for your figure, particularly for the bosom, it drops you see. And the curves begin to bulge where they should properly billow. No hard labour for me. One must remember there things if one proposes to live forever. One slip young man- and one may well be dead'. She went to the bookcase and took down a small volume. She held it out to Charles.

'Here- you must read this book, it's all about my life. So convenient to have it handy. If I forget something, and I must confess that I sometimes do forget things, any important episodes or even the tiniest detail is recorded here. I can just look it up. It's all there. You may borrow it but be very careful not to lose it- it's my whole life you understand.' The book Charles saw, was a biography of Edmund Campion the Elizabethan Jesuit martyr, by Evelyn Waugh. He was spared a reply by the sound of someone entering the house.

The woman who now came into the room was handsome rather than beautiful. Her eyes deep set and very blue were her best features. Her hair was grey and cut in a severe short bob which did little for her heart shaped face and flawless pink and white complexion. 'English Rose' came to Charles Huxley's mind. In her hands she carried a large box which she set down on a table. Charles, whose thinking had been put severely out of joint, again held out his hand like a drowning man to his savior. She took it in her cold one and smiled, 'Dr. Huxley of course. I am Clarissa Hare Bell, I do apologies for my absence, I should have been here to greet you, its unforgivable of me. I'm so happy…' Her eyes belied the sentiment as they rested on Mae West but she remained unruffled '…that you're finally here. I guess you've met my Mother, my husband's mother that is. She should not be here, she should be having her nap.' She turned to Mae West and said very kindly as to a small and recalcitrant child, 'Run upstairs now Elizabeth dear- I'll find Steve- she'll help you undress.'

Charles watched in silence as Clarissa stepped through the French window into the garden and called, 'Steve…Steve… where are you

Steve?' Mae West seized the moment, 'So you're a Doctor- being a Doctor I am sure you have just been made aware of this intolerable behaviour towards poor little Mae West. It goes on and on, the nagging never stops. Time for your nap- time for your tea, time for whatever they say- always telling me what to do, treating me like a child- even calling me Elizabeth for God's sake- you can see that it's intolerable- and as well as that- quite unforgivable.'

She moved closer to Charles and whispering now went on, 'I think they're trying to get rid of me, all the signs of conspiracy are there. But they will find it quite impossible. You see I'm indestructible- I'm the eternal, the immortal sex symbol.' She laughed roguishly and then as a very pretty young woman entered the room with Clarissa, she put her hands up to hide her mouth like a naughty child caught out in a prank and wailed, 'Oh God- here he is- my jailer,' Mae West moved to hide behind Charles, still whispering, 'Oh dear, oh dear I do hope he won't beat me…' 'Come along now Elizabeth, up we go to bed, you really must have your nap.' Steve's voice was calm as her demeanor gentle. 'I'm so sorry Clarissa- we went for a walk up to the Hall to see the children and she gave me the slip. Come along now angel, up to bed- you must have your nap or you won't be allowed to go to the party tonight.'

'Oh the party- I forgot.' Elizabeth clapped her hands, 'Goody, goody, a party, a party, a lovely party,' whatever shall I wear?'

'That's enough now angel, quite enough. You mustn't overdo it- say goodbye to the gentleman.'

'Goodbye- goodbye-' Mae West waved prettily 'but as I always say- too much of a good thing can be wonderful.'

She gave Charles a last beguiling smile, 'Remember- I'm no angel.'

The grotesque apparition allowed herself to be led away.

CHAPTER TWO

'Look' said Clarissa 'from this window you have a perfect view of the Hare Bell Hall'. Charles looked and was again enchanted. So this was England, England as he had not dared to imagine it. Hare Bell Hall set in green acres of parkland beneath distant wooded hills lacked only a moat to realise the palatial edifice of his dreams.

'Truly a magnificent building', he said and felt his words inadequate.

'I think you will be quite comfortable here' Clarissa searched the bedroom for flaws but Mrs. Jenkins had not let her down. The mirror above the washstand was spotless, the cushions on the small sofa beneath the window properly plumped, and on the table a vase full of yellow roses perfumed the air.

'The horsehair mattress on your bed originated from those austere Victorian days has, fortunately for you, been replaced. I slept on it once and found it unbearably scratchy.'

Charles nodded, it was all he could think of to do. 'Our bedroom is across the hall, Elizabeth and Steve have a room each in the turret, and you will be glad to hear we have two bathrooms- a luxury I insisted upon when we moved into the Gate House.

'I'm sure I will be fine in here- the room is great, just great...' further accolades escaped him. He found he could only smile broadly.

'Why don't you settle in and then come on downstairs.'

Clarissa left him alone and made her way downstairs. The man was a disappointment. Americans were generally reputed to be loud, brash and self-confident. On first impressions she found Dr. Huxley unforthcoming and inarticulate. In the letters they had exchanged prior to this visit he had seemed quite different. More outgoing and certainly more lively. Of course his intelligence and intimate knowledge of his subject may have made him somewhat depressed, even austere. Or perhaps he was suffering for jet lag. It did not occur to her that Basil's mother in her role of Mae West might have silenced him. Clarissa began to regret the machinations she had set in motion.

In the walled garden behind the rhododendron walk Sir Basil Hare Bell pushed Steve hard up against the espaliered pear and fondled her breasts through the oatmeal Marks and Spencer tracksuit she was wearing. Before long he slipped a hand under the top which came away easily from the trousers. Soon one of his impatient hands slipped under the white sports bra (also M. & S.) and fastened onto her naked breast. The other delved eagerly in her oatmeal track suit pants as the espaliered pear gnawed at her back.

'Take them off,' he whispered. Steve, breathing hard pushed him away.

'Stop it Bas, not now, someone's just arrived. An American. He's going to be in the yellow room- the one with the extensive views over the Park.'

'Oh my God, he's here already…' Sir Basil reluctantly removed his hands from Steve's soft young body. He signed. And mopped his face with a handkerchief.

'God only knows what Clarissa has in mind inviting that fellow. Oh well, I suppose we'd better get on with our jogging, we ought to work up a swear one way or another.'

'Oh yes- a healthy mind in a healthy body is hard to beat.'

'I'll race you to the Hall and back- winner takes all.'

From his window in the yellow room Charles Huxley saw the two tiny figures moving quickly across the green sward of the perfectly manicured garden. They looked like puppets in a toy landscape. An English landscape.

Clarissa poured tea into delicately flowered cups.

'Milk?'

'Yes please.'

'Sugar?'

No thank you.'

'What a polite young man you are not a bit like Americans are usually portrayed.' When Charles looked surprised she added, 'But then you've been to Harvard have you not? I suppose that makes the difference.' Charles once again could think of no reply so sipped his tea trying not to slurp. It would not do to shatter his image so soon.

'My husband should be here presently- he's out jogging. He seems to think the exercise will prolong his life.'

As if on cue Sir Basil Hare Bell, rather red and sweaty, appeared at the French window.

'Ah- there you are Basil. This is Dr. Charles Huxley.'

'So you are the mysterious Dr. Huxley' said Basil shaking his hand, 'Clarissa could not be persuaded to reveal a thing about you except your name. Tell me are you a Doctor of medicine?' 'No Sir Basil- I have a Ph. D.' 'Then that surely means you are an expert of some kind- all Americans with Ph. D's are experts are they not, or certainly specialists of something or another. What is your specialty Dr. Huxley?'

'Well...um...it's a long story.' Charles looked helplessly at Clarissa.

'It's a surprise Basil, you'll hear later tonight. Shouldn't you go up and change?'

'All in good time my dear. Just now a cup of tea would be acceptable. I need reviving. You see Dr. Huxley I've been jogging. Do you jog? I find it a most stimulating pastime.

If you exercise in that manner we have twenty acres of parkland here at your disposal.' 'No I don't jog- believe me Sir Basil jogging has it's perils. May I suggest that you don't overdo it- you could run into trouble.'

'Run into trouble- that's very good.' Sir Basil laughed shortly, he loathed puns, 'I do not agree Dr. Huxley. I've been jogging for six months now and I feel so well it can only be good for me. I'm fitter than I've been for years.' Clarissa handed him a cup. 'Basil imagines jogging will bring him, if not quite immortality then at least life-long indestructibility. I say it will kill him.'

'Nonsense Clarissa- don't be so negative. Statistics tell me that I will live, on average, three years longer than non-joggers.'

'On a time basis Basil that means you will spend those three extra bonus years jogging. What a frightful waste of time.'

'That rather depends on ones philosophy of time and how one wastes it, does it not my dear,' asked Basil. The question did not require an answer. Charles felt an increased tension in the exchange.

'I hope you will be comfortable with us Dr. Huxley,' Basil remembered his manners.

'We are not as grand here as at the big house but times change. My son Zil and his family live at the Hall now, much more sensible since there are so many of them. The name Zil by the way is short for Basil. All eldest sons of the Hare Bells are compelled by tradition to be named Basil. Zil and his wife Teresa have four children and are expecting another. I believe we're dining there tonight are we not Clarissa?'

'Yes Basil- at eight sharp. We must be on time tonight, we mustn't upset cook. Teresa can't afford to lose her now that the baby is due. Overdue in fact. But Charles doesn't want to know about our domestic arrangements do you?'

'I...I...' Charles bogged down. He did not realise the question was rhetorical. He was finding English conversation not only extremely difficult to follow but unsettling to his logical American mind. Basil smiled. It was obvious that Charles Huxley was not at ease. So far, although not actively disliking the man (even though he was an American and Americans as the old Duke used to say, were all savages)

7

he was, as far as Basil is concerned, on probation. Time would tell what he was made of. He said, 'I'll be very pleased to show you around the Dr. Huxley if a mixture of architectural styles interests you.'

'I'd like that a lot Sir Basil.'

'The Hall has been in my family for seven generations and I trust will remain in it for at least seven more.'

The glance exchange between Clarissa and Charles was suddenly intimate. All at once Basil felt uneasy. On his way upstairs to change he was overcome with a sense of foreboding, a feeling that Charles Huxley's visit foreshadowed a significant and threatening change- perhaps to his whole way of life. But he shrugged off the premonition- he could deal with any American Clarissa liked to serve up- he would eat him for breakfast like a well-scrambled egg. As he ran his bath he smiled at his little joke.

The kitchen of the Hall was old-fashioned, large and draughty. Cook spread dripping generously over the shoulder of mutton watched by three small girls.

'If mother catches you doing that she'll be very cross' said Harriet. Father isn't allowed fat, he's on a diet.'

'He'll never know and neither will she- not if you don't tell her.' Cook put the dripping she concealed in an empty baked bean can under the sink.

'But we will tell her, we will...'

'What about a jam tart for each of you- look there, I baked them fresh this morning and put in that lovely raspberry jam made by Mr. Crabtree and his wife Evelyn.' Cook laughed merrily at her little joke and handed out the forbidden carbohydrates and white death (sugar.)

'Not then not a word to Bessie'

'Who's Bessie?'

'Don't be silly Henry,' Harriet was scornful 'it's just a saying. Cook means us not to tell Mother.'

'I wasn't going to tell anyway' said Henrietta through a mouthful of jam tart. 'I never tell. Only you tell Harry, you tell all the time.'

'That's enough of that now' said Cook 'anyone who spills the beans about what goes on in my kitchen won't get any more jam tarts or anything else nice for that matter.' She began to open cans of green peas and put the contents into a saucepan, the peas were not particularly green, they emerged with more of a greyish hue.

'Mother doesn't like peas out of a tin,' said Harriet the spokesperson for the prosecution.

Chapter Two

'Doesn't she now,' said Cook reaching into the pantry for a can of beetroot. 'What she doesn't know won't hurt her.' 'Harry will spill the beans,' said Edwina, 'I bet she will.' 'Not if she knows what's good for her.'

Harriet took the last jam tart. Cook pretended not to notice. She continued, 'At least I don't have to make a cake- Lady Clarissa has ordered one from Mrs. Payne in the village.'

'Will we be allowed to have some cake too- please Cook?' 'If there's any left over I'll keep some for you.' 'Promise?' 'Harriet fixed her with a blackmailer's eye. 'Cross my heart.' Cook emptied the beetroot onto a plate.

'Now when you've finished your tarts you can help me set the table. Big party tonight, dinner for eight.' She sighed. 'That's not very many,' said Harriet.

'It is when you're all on your own, and it's a long way to the dining room' said Cook 'I don't get much help around here you know.'

'Well that's your job. That's what mother always says.' Harriet was not Cook's favourite child. 'Go on upstairs now, Nanny'll be looking for you. You don't want to let her catch you with those jammy mouths.' 'What are we going to have for our supper tonight?' asked Harriet.

'It's in the pantry all ready for you. Nanny made it specially. Lovely grated carrot sandwiches on lovely tasty, brown bread.' Cook invariably had her revenge.

'Zil,' the very pregnant Teresa wailed 'how can I be expected to entertain so many people in my condition?' She was lying on a green velvet chaise longue, a cup of tea on the table beside her, the Harper's and Queen on her lap, or on the little that was left of her lap.' Zil patted her dark head, 'Darling it's Clarissa's birthday- you must.' 'Must I? Can't I be ill or something?' 'No.' 'If you hadn't invited the vicar- with Steve that makes eight at the table.'

'We must occasionally reward the vicar with an invitation my darling- do remember how useful the man is; think of all those christenings. And you know how he adores visiting the gentry as he calls us. I know you can handle it.'

'I don't want to handle anything, I just want to sleep. And I certainly don't want to handle the vicar- he's so old-fashioned and such an awful snob. And if he tells the story of how he gave up smoking once more I will kill myself- at the table- I mean it. I will stab myself to death with one of your mothers crested forks.'

9

'My love we all know how hard this pregnancy has been for you but you must make an effort, Just think- in another week we will have our son.'

'You hope.' Teresa did not sound convinced. There were four girls in the nursery- noisy testaments to Zil's unswerving ambition to produce a son and heir for Hare Bell Hall. 'And now Nanny has taken umbrage because she isn't allowed to dine with us- but I can't have the children running wild can I?'

'No darling, of course you can't.'

'What id she leaves me- what will I do- and with the new baby arriving any minute…'

'She won't leave…' now Zil sounded unconvinced.' But if she does we'll fin another nanny- I promise.'

CHAPTER THREE

'She's dotty of course but quite harmless. Marvellous for 85 years old.' Clarissa and Charles were walking along a wide avenue bordered by clipped yew hedges on their way towards the Hall. Charles carried the box containing the birthday cake. Clarissa continued, 'Elizabeth was always lively and so active and energetic. She never seemed to think about old age at all- at least she never mentioned it and then suddenly on her 80th birthday it hit her. Wham- something snapped- she was old. The realisation caused her to sink into decline and the optimistic, vivacious woman she had been vanished as though by magic. It was terribly sad- we tried everything- counseling, doctors, psychiatrists but nothing helped. She refused to speak, she often stayed alone in her room, leaving it only at meal times until one day she found a biography of Mae West in Basil's library at the Hall. After that there was no holding her back- she lives the role. I do hope you didn't find her to startling.'

'No, oh no, of course not...' lied Charles bravely.

'A pity really she was such a dear and now... I blame Basil, he encourages her, though perhaps he's right to do so; she seems happy enough.'

'But how does she manage to look the part...I mean it's amazing...her appearance.' Charles wondered if he had gone to far.

'That's easy. When she was young in the mad twenties she often dressed as Mae West. They had endless fancy dress parties in those days- dressing up was extrapolated into an art form. The clothes were all there, packed in trunks stored up in the attics at the Hall. Elizabeth was rather like Basil- she never threw anything out, so there they were- costumes for any and every occasion. She was quite a wild young thing you know- fast cars, bizarre parties, she was a friend of the Mitford girls of course.'

Charles nodded, the only way he could convey his fascination with the story. He thought fleetingly of his own mother back in the States, undoubtedly less flamboyant, less interesting but certainly caring and certainty not as made as Elizabeth. An ordinary, normal American mother who baked an apple pie many would envy. Right now he missed her.

Clarissa continued, 'It does mean that we must have a series of minders for Elizabeth- I say a series because of course they never stay long. Young girls have better things to do than to look after senile old ladies.'

In the distance three small girls broke away from a woman wheeling a pram in their direction and ran towards them. The tallest flung herself at Clarissa.

'Clarissa, Clarissa do you know what Cook did?' 'Now Harry darling- no tales.' To Charles she said, 'These are my granddaughters, Harry, Henry and Eddie. Georgie is in the pram. Say hello to Dr. Huxley girls.'

The girls mumbled shy greetings and Charles said, 'Hello there, hallo, hi there...' the fabled American eloquence had yet to put in an appearance, his jogging quip to date the only and meagre evidence of a sense of humour. Clarissa again sighed inwardly. But the children turned to him with interest.

'You're from off the telly- you're from Sesame Street.' 'They are only allowed to watch educational T.V.' said Clarissa, 'their mother I am glad to say is terribly strict.'

'Come along girls, time for your bath.' Nanny turned for home pushing the enormous baby carriage with decision. This splendid machine had no doubt harboured all the Hare Bell babies for seemingly a multitude of generations since the wheels rolled with a decided squeak. Practical Charles longed for an oil can.

'Will we be allowed some birthday cake, please Clarissa, please...'

'Of course- I promise to keep you some but not a word to your mother.'

They walked along companionably together, the Hall looming larger as they approached. It was a square building of three lofty storeys with a double flight of beautifully proportioned windows. Four stately chimneys rose about the roof in the middle of which the cracks in the lead of the cupola glittered in the weak sunlight. It was obvious that the Hall was still in much need of repair.

'And there,' Clarissa pointed 'is the famous Hare Bell fountain.'

The rhododendron walk led them towards a large circular fountain, situated below the parterres (now largely overgrown) and enclosed by balustrades overlooking the further view of the park. In the centre of the fountain stood a number of recognisable figures. Neptune blowing into a conch, Mercury the winged messenger poised for take off on an obscure mission and a number of mermaids dressed in flowing, mid-Victorian stone gowns.

'How pretty' said Charles 'does it work, I mean...' 'Unfortunately only sometimes,' said Clarissa 'it is fed by an ingenious but regrettably uncertain water cistern. The fountain was installed in 1853 to celebrate the 200th anniversary of the building of the Hall. We call it Old Leaky because that's all it ever seems to be able to accomplish with any style.' There was in fact water dribbling out of Neptune's mossy green conch into the muddy water below.

'It would be very difficult as well as expensive to restore the fountain to proper working order. It's one of the most important items on Basil's list of restorations, if he can ever afford it.' Clarissa laughed ironically, intimating that this was an unlikely event in the near or even distant future.

As they approached the Hall an aged black and white spaniel came lumbering towards them, fluffy tall wagging.

Around its neck drooped a huge pink ribbon.

'Look Clarissa, Daisy's got a ribbon on for your birthday. I tied it myself.'

'Oh darling Harry- how thoughtful. Isn't he a gorgeous thing then.' Clarissa dropped to her knees and patted the dog which responded with much licking of her face.

Fastidious Charles watched in dismay as the dog finished washing Clarissa's face and began to lick the faces of the children one by one.

'Poor old Daisy is part of the family. We got him as a puppy about fifteen years ago. He's much older than the girls aren't you Daisy?' she lowered her voice to a whisper, 'God only knows what will happen when he dies, the children will be inconsolable.' The over plump Daisy attempted to jump on Charles, an unsuccessful effort which he silently applauded. He was not found of dogs, particularly not of smelly old spaniels. Clarissa continued, 'The Hare Bells have always had spaniels, it's an ancient tradition. In the old days, when there was shooting here, they were working dogs of course. Retrievers.'

'Daisy can chase a ball and catch it,' Eddie told him proudly. 'Not any more he can't dear' said Clarissa, 'he's too old and arthritic.' To Charles, Harry said, 'Like old Mae, she's so old she can hardly get up the stairs now- and you know something?'

'Now what could that be,' Charles prided himself on his way with children. 'She's an addict.' Clarissa frowned. 'Well that's what Basil says anyways.'

Once again Charles necessarily remained speechless. 'Harry is our insufferable little know-it-all- time for tea now isn't it?', Clarissa looked meaningfully at Nanny who squared her shoulders.

'That's enough now children- say goodbye to Granny and to the nice man.' Clarissa squirmed. Granny was a forbidden word but Nanny invariably ignored the order. She disapproved heartily of children using the proper names of their elders and betters. Clarissa was a grandmother and 'Granny; if Nanny has anything to do with it, she would be called.

For Clarissa there were no countermeasures. Teresa had decreed that Nanny like Cook must be appeased at any cost. Cooks and Nannys were as scarce as hens teeth said Teresa and as difficult to keep.

'Goodbye Granny...' Harry grinned cheekily at Clarissa. The other two echoed 'Goodbye Granny.' Thus Nanny triumphant, the squeaking pram and the children moved off and disappeared into a side door of the Hall, Daisy the spaniel from this angle quite visibly a male animal, lumbering along behind them.

Clarissa and Charles took the birthday cake into the kitchen where Cook was putting the finishing touches to the tinned salmon. She was arranging the grey and pink matter on eight wilted lettuce leaves lying prostrate on eight priceless Limoges plates.

'Oh cook, Dr. Huxley and I will leave cake in the pantry,' said Clarissa 'and then we'll just slip away- we musn't disturb you at your artistic endeavours.' Cook beamed.

'Now Dr. Huxley- it's time to go back to the Gate House to change for my birthday dinner.' Clarissa led the way back along the rhododendron walk.

'Lady Clarissa please don't stand on ceremony- do call me Charles.'

'You Americans - if anything it would have to be Lady Hare Bell but I insist on plain Clarissa. After our long correspondence over these past months I feel I know you very well indeed.' Clarissa lied easily, it was an essential part of the way she had been brought up. She went on, 'There is one thing I am dying to ask you- tell me do they by any chance call you Chuck? I understand that is the fate of the name Charles in the States.'

'It's certainly a common contraction at home' said Charles but not in my case. Though I must admit that at college I was known as Hux.'

'I like that- I shall call you Hux and you must call me Clarissa. I can't tell you how relieved I am that you're not a Chuck – I don't think I could have borne that. The thought has been haunting me for months. Now go and change Hux and when you've finished come down to the drawing room and we'll have a drink together before we set off for the Hall. Basil will drive us- it's too dark to walk all that way at night, and you have all your equipment.'

'Fine,' said Charles 'I'll have it all ready by then.' Did the man drink, was Clarissa's next thought. That was the next discovery to be made. Many of these Americans were such prudes- nothing stronger than that disgusting iced tea they all seemed to favour. 'Sounds good to me,' said Charles. Thank heaven for that, thought Clarissa.

In the yellow room Charles unpacked his clothes and put them neatly into drawers and cupboards. Closets as he thought of them. The twilight view from his window, purple clouds massing in the distance promising rain, reflected his mood. Homesickness already. He felt like a small boy thrust into the new milieu of a boarding school; his euphoria for all things English fast evaporating. Nothing he had read had prepared him for this experience. Although, he suddenly remembered there was one book which he should, perhaps have taken more seriously- Alice's adventures in Wonderland. There was a certain logic there, a familiarity. 'Alice had got so much into the way of expecting nothing but out of the way things to happen, this it seemed quite dull and stupid for life to go on in the common way.' And 'Curioiser and curiouser…' that made sense- he felt sure he had experienced only the beginnings of extraordinary happenings. Clarissa in her letters had appeared to be so normal, so warm and caring. Yet she seemed in the flesh to be rather cold even casual; she had been quite brusque with her husband, one could almost infer dismissive. However his own and Clarissa's was to be merely a business relationship. He would do well to remember that fact he told himself sternly. No more open mouthed gaping; accept things as they are at this moment- as did Alice he told himself. Do the business you came to do in this strange land and be gone as fast as possible. At that moment he heard a scuffling in the hall beyond his door. Uncoordinated footsteps, giggling, more scuffling, laughter and a voice, unmistakably Sir Basil's whispering 'not now Steve… take your hot little hands off me… wait you naughty girl…you must wait.' The giggling and the footsteps proceeded towards the stairs which led up to the turret rooms. Charles turned away from the door to which he had been drawn by what could only be described as seriously sensuous horse play, shaking his head, no longer in disbelief, but in bemused acceptance of further untoward events.

Outside the rain began to patter down. A typical English drizzle, a thin drizzle. He watched as it fell gently on the improbably picturesque English Countryside.

Clarissa at her dressing table looked at her reflection with distaste.

'Old…old…old…' she told it. She brushed the cropped greying hair away from her face. Should she perhaps grow it longer? Should she dye it? She banished the thought even as she heard her mother stirring in the grave.

'Be your age Clarissa, grow old with decorum,' she heard her mother's voice as though she were in the room standing behind her at the dressing table. Her mother continued, 'Nice girls do not dye their hair Clarissa- never contemplate such a waywardness as the dyeing of your hair. You will be known as fast.' Even in her coffin Mother was hopelessly old- fashioned. But Clarissa felt her hair needed something…what? Come to that so did her face. She seriously needed a new face- an impossible dream.

She fastened the beautiful oval Hare Belle pearls into her ears where they swung gracefully. The pearls, bequeathed to the family by one of the original Basil Hare Bells- the buccaneer Hare Bell- pirate probably and misappropriate no doubt in the Caribbean, so the story went, had been handed down from generation to generation of Hare Bell women. At least their luminosity deepened the colour of Clarissa's eyes. She gazed again at her reflection, resigned but only for the moment, to her lot. For now that Charles was here, there was hope, there was a possibility of chance.

CHAPTER FOUR

Numerous clocks were striking six as Charles entered the drawing room. He was alone. How clever he thought as he listened to the many chiming's, to be able to make so many clocks strike at the same time. 'Isn't it an amazing feat' said Clarissa as she came into the room carrying a silver ice bucket, 'to have all the clocks striking at the same moment. It's all Basil's work; he winds them for me and sets them to the correct time every day. I used to collect clocks; many more of mine are up at the Hall but they are never wound- Teresa and Zil could not stand the noise. They said the children weren't able to get to sleep. A pity really. I think clocks make a lovely noise, despite reminding one of the passing of time as they tick, tick, tick, tock. Now then, what will you have to drink?' She really looked splendid thought Charles. The blue silk gown matched her eyes and the pearls in her ears set off her beautifully English complexion. 'Do you have such a thing as a dry martini?'

'Certainly- and I'll join you. Perhaps you would mix it, Hux I'm sure you can do a better job than Basil usually does- he's always too mean with the gin.'

In his white dress shirt with the wing collar, the tartan tie and matching triangles (two) of handkerchief peeping out of the breast pocket of his dark blue dinner jacket Charles looked, thought Clarissa like an American film star arriving at the Dorothy Chandler Pavilion for the annual presentation of the Academy Awards.

Too- awful- tawdry. But she had to admit that he was in fact rather handsome, the tartan tie (no doubt a mistaken obeisance to all things supposedly English) notwithstanding.

She opened the magnificent old French armoire in which the drinks were kept.

'There you are Hux,' she handed him the ice, 'everything is here including glasses on the bottom shelf. Go to it.'

Charles happily mixed and stirred, placed olives in two glasses and finally poured.

'Try this,' he said. Clarissa sipped. 'Delicious. You are clever Hux. As I predicted these martinis are much nicer than Basil's. By the way he won't be joining us, he's having his nap.' Charles sipped silently and with an effort banished from his mind the recent scene outside his bedroom door.

'Lately Basil has become terribly obsessed with his health,' continued Clarissa, 'He jogs like mad, as you saw earlier, swallows thousands of restorative pills of some curious sort and takes these little naps- to restore his nervous energy is how he puts it. Trying unsuccessfully to restore his vanished youth is how I put it. But do sit down, Hux, I am so glad you are here at last.' Charles summoned courage, 'A very happy birthday to you Clarissa- and I am very happy too, to be here at last. You know it was your char lady who told me it was your birthday today.'

'Oh dear- you musn't call Mrs. Jenkins a char lady, that term is not only out of date but politically incorrect. She is only, as no doubt she told you, doing me a favour. But I don't know what I'd do without her.'

'Yes she told me- she's well aware of her value. But I do wish I'd known. I would have brought you a gift.'

'Don't be silly Hux. What you're about to do for me is a gift enough. I simply thought that my birthday was an especially appropriate occasion to break the news to the whole family. You see they have to put on a good show- happy faces only- it's a rule we have. No bad tempers and no sulking on birthdays. Desperately necessary in the circumstances I feel.'

'So nobody knows anything about our venture?'

'Nobody. And therefore I'm feeling very apprehensive.'

'But Clarissa you let me to believe we had Sir Basil's approval.'

'I had to do that Hux, to make sure you would come. But don't worry; we'll break it to him, to all of them, gently. When I say we, I really mean you Hux. Because you will be able to explain it all so much more intelligently than I ever could. In any case Basil and Zil never listen to me.' Dismayed, Charles said, 'But this makes it very awkward for me...' I know Hux, please forgive me- you see unfortunately it's all a matter of money.'

'I guess it always is.' Charles sighed, this was going to be more difficult than he had imagined.

'But Clarissa, you assured me you had the money.' 'Believe me Hux I do have the money and that's just the problem. It's my own money. Up to now Basil has had no reason to suppose I wouldn't go on giving money to him for the upkeep and restoration of his precious Hall. That is what I have been doing for years. Our proposition will put an end to that.'

Charles felt the rug slipping from under his feet. He brought the pitcher of martinis to Clarissa, 'Another drink?'

'Please Hux.' Clarissa held out her glass gratefully. She could see the bewilderment on his face. Charles gave himself a refill and gulped rather than sipped. It was a damn good martini and right now he needed it. With this new information to be taken on board, with dinner to be faced, with the entire proposition to be explained to the whole unsuspecting and probably hostile family, an overwhelming feeling of importance overcame him.

'Clarissa, I guess we'd better call the whole thing off.' 'Oh Hux-no, please don't say that.' Clarissa had been right to distrust the man. He was a wimp after all. 'We can't give up now Hux. You're here, you've got all your equipment with you and you know I've set my heart on it don't you?' She looked appealing at Charles, her very blue eyes harbouring the glint of a tear. 'Will Sir Basil be very angry Clarissa? I'm not very brave you know.' A coward was how Clarissa would have put it. She squeezed out a tear.

Upstairs, in one of the small turret rooms Sir Basil Hare Bell was actively and in the interest only of his health, engaged in restoring his lost youth. A rosy breathless Steve slide off his naked body, nipping his ear playfully as she did so.

'Wow Bas, the was terrific.' Basil too winded to reply placed one hand over his pounding heart, the other on one of the delicious paler spots on Steve's body. Most of her smooth skin was coloured an even café-au-lait acquired on her annual holiday in Spain. The pale spots were not large, Steve's bathers being more in the nature of colourful bits of string than reasonable body covering. Basil was able to fully appreciate and enjoy the delectable contrast. He stroked the lovely length of her smooth back and signed with pleasure. Steve sighing too asked, 'What's the time, my love?' Basil looked at his watch, the only thing he was wearing and said, 'Time for one more you lucky duck.'

'You see Hux, I must tell you the only thing that really matters to Basil s the Hall.' Clarissa, encouraged by her second martini had decided to tell Charles Huxley at least some of the truth. 'The Hall dates back to 1653 when it was completed by the first Basil Hare Bell, who was translated to Baronet in 1660 by your namesake Charles the Second as reward for his loyalty and help in the restoration of the monarchy and it's been in the family ever since. In the middle of the 18th century they nearly lost it- there was a profligate elder son who squandered money, gambling I believe, and allowed the whole estate to run down very badly. The Hall fell into disrepair but fortunately the next heir pulsed several rabbits out of various hats and began to process of rebuilding. The rabbits according to the family history were some exquisitely devious dealings in the market place, however ends justify means in Hare Bell philosophy.

Since then it's been not only a matter of restoration but also of day-to-day expenses. Such a large house required constant attention; even the basic upkeep is enormous, rates, taxes and so on. And over the years I have provided a great deal of the money.' She held out her glass for more of the perfect martini. Charles willingly refilled it. Thus heartened Clarissa took a deep breath, 'You see Hux, you must understand that Basil only married me for my money. He married me to ensure the future of the Hall- a trite story is it not, but quite a common one as you will doubtless remember. Many of your compatriots married into the aristocracy here- uniting European style with transatlantic funds is how I've heard that type of merger described'. Charles dimly remembered stories of such marriages, remembered more clearly the stories of the disastrous disintegrations of many of these ill-fated unions. He instantly became concerned. 'Clarissa is Sir Basil cruel- has he ill-treated you?' 'No Hux, not at all, it's nothing like that. We get on rather well most of the time. You know he's even quite fond of me in his own way but he does exactly as he pleases with little reference to me. It's his dream to see the Hall completely restored and brought back to its original condition, its original splendor. This is really all he cares about- to see his son and his son's son possessors of the Hall- a Hall in perfect condition. The continuity is what matters- the stretch of the years behind him like the tail of a comet and lasting as long as eternity. Living in the Hall is not important to him. He prefers to be in the Gate house where he can actually see it, whole and eventually perfect, before him'.

'Did you know all that before you married him?'

'Oh yes- it has all been entirely my own fault. My father warned me but I was not prepared to listen, although I suspected even that Basil wasn't quite as made about me as I was about him. But I married him because I loved him. I wanted to help with the Hall, I wanted to make him happy. Fortunately my father was rather harder headed than I was and tied my money up so that I couldn't give it all away at once. That is probably the only reason I'm still here- the money is mine and I dole it out whenever Basil, or rather the Hall, needs it.'

Once again Charles was silent. To Clarissa's story there was no answer. She could see the pity in his eyes.

'Above all please don't feel sorry for me Hux. It was my choice to marry Basil and I've had to make the best of it. Now we'll see how he copes with something that won't suit him quite so well. It should be quite a revelation. You will go through with our plan won't you Hux?'

Chapter Four

'Clarissa now that I know what you have endured, I mean… now that I understand…of course I will. You can count on me for sure- and that's a promise.'

In the turret room Basil and Steve awoke from their brief reviving sleep. 'Now I really must go and get Elizabeth dressed for dinner tonight,; said Steve 'and you should dress too. It's Clarissa's birthday after all. You know Bas she's such a sweetie you should be nicer to her.'

'I'm perfectly nice to her- I don't beat her do I?' 'Oh Bas don't be horrid. You know what I mean. If I didn't know that she was hopelessly frigid and has been avoiding lovemaking in any form ever since you married her I wouldn't be here at all. I respect Clarissa, you do know that don't you Bas?' Basil stroked the damp blonde curls away from her face, 'You are a dear and lovable girl, do you know that?' Steve put her arms around him, 'And you are my poor precious neglected little baby,' A comparison which had more to do with Steve's caring nature than with the truth. She dropped a series of small kisses on his cheek. Basil sighed contentedly.

Steve was a nice girl. A simple, helpful, efficient, easily duped, healthy girl and jolly in bed. Basil had learned a lot from Steve who was an expert, and not only in that particular field. He appreciated her undoubted qualities enormously. He patted her round and silky bottom, 'Off you go then- go and do your duty.'

CHAPTER FIVE

Sherry was served in the salon before dinner. It was the room the family used most often since it commanded sweeping views of the terraced gardens and hills beyond. A large room it was decorated in styles plundered from three centuries and although the result was rather undisciplined it was nevertheless comfortable. Teresa's hand was visible in the occasional Laura Ashley print cushion and an odd armchair or two covered in flowered chintz. Charles was introduced to Teresa and Zil; Teresa, whose pregnancy was clearly overwhelming her, welcomed him graciously and then returned to the severe upright chair from which she had struggled into an upright position and which appeared to be scant panacea for her overladen back. Zil, a shorter edition of his father though with more and much darker hair, shook his hand firmly and offered sherry- an amontillado, a sweet, or a Tio Pepe.

'I recommend the Tio Pepe Hux,' said Clarissa 'I imagine you are not familiar with sherry, am I right?' 'Sherry is not as popular in the States as it is here,' replied Charles politely, 'but I will take your advice.' He wondered why the English assumed that Americans knew nought of English customs, ironically, as he knew of course that Sherry was in fact Spanish wine. He wondered too how the sherry would mix with the three martinis. 'What a cunning little bow tie,' Basil waved his glass in the direction of Charles' neck, 'Your family tartan perhaps?' Bewildered, Charles smiled vaguely. He had no idea that Basil was getting at him. 'Rodeo Drive actually,' he said. Clarissa clapped, 'Touché Basil. And leave poor Hux alone. Go help Steve- here she comes with Elizabeth.'

Tonight Mae West was splendidly adorned in black velvet, sumptuously decorated with multi-coloured, sparkling sequins. She carried an enormous ostrich feather fan which she wielded with abandon.

'I'm the bad girl of Broadway,' she told the assembled company, 'I climbed the ladder of success wrong by wrong.' 'Whatever you do don't laugh' Clarissa whispered to Charles, 'it encourages her to even greater excesses.' Basil dodging errant feathers placed the colourful figure in an armchair. 'Sit down and be quiet please mother, or you'll be taken straight off to bed.' Elizabeth frowned petulantly, waved her fan about and muttered.

'Bed..bed... I believe I've spent a great deal of my time in bed- that is a quite jolly pastime you know... I could tell you many of my adventures, all with the most handsomest of men, and all film starts, as we used to call them…' 'Yes mother your stories are always so endlessly fascinating but just now that is quite enough. Do remember that we have guests.' Basil fixed her with a stern look and Elizabeth at least subsided.

'Ah, here is your Vicar- Cannon Moffitt.' Zil hurried forward to greet a short, stout man with profuse and greying curls framing a small, round, pixie face, who entered with outstretched hand and a broad smile. He was wearing ecclesiastical evening dress which had clearly seen better days. The ancient tall coat was a rusty black, his polished dog collar yellowing around the edges and the black silk front sported an odd hole here and there through which a white under vest was visible. After introductions to the new face and the greeting of his hosts was done he fixed his attention upon Charles.

'I hear you are from America Dr. Huxley- a wonderful land, wonderful. I have never visited there- so far away, so foreign, not my cup of tea at all.' Clutching a glass of sweet sherry to his breasts he gazed at Charles as though observing the last surviving member of an almost extinct species of exotic birds. He was earnestly, 'But I must tell you that my late wife, when she was alive was very fond of something called a Big Mac. Whenever we drove to out neighbouring village on a business of one kind or another, funerals mostly, she insisted that we visit the establishment at which this particular delicacy was available. An American delicacy I believe.'

Charles gaped. Was it possible to be so out of touch with the realities of life? He was spared a reply by Cook who appeared at the door, banging a gong with a brio attributable to an impulsion of repressed fury, 'Dinner is served.' She snapped.

'Oh dear,' Teresa struggled out of her chair, 'we must go in immediately or there will be hell to pay. Cook is doing me a huge favour. Do please bring your sherries- they will go well with the soup.' Where were the faithful old retainers who served the family willingly, humbly, silently and with perpetual and unswerving loyalty wondered Charles.

Non-existent here at Hare Bell Hall it seemed. The universal quest for equality in modern life, that equality which makes the exigencies of life a burden for all equally, had penetrated even this venerable mansion.

The dining table had been set in the Great Hall, in honour of Clarissa's birthday, Basil explained to Charles as he pointed out some of the features of the magnificent space which rose to two storeys of the house- the fine wooden ceiling supported by elaborately carved beams and the famous wood paneling carved by Grinling Gibbons in 1714.

On the walls hung two beautifully worked French tapestries in colours of deep blue and white and gold and many portraits of dead ancestors in heavily gilded frames.

They sat beneath this splendor in draughty discomfort. The soup was already on the table as they took their seats and already cold. 'The soup is called Brown Windsor,' explained Clarissa, 'A traditional English soup.' It was certainly brown, and being cold, quite horrible. They lifted their spoons, Charles after the first mouthful with a certain timidity.

'My dear Teresa,' said the vicar genially 'when is the baby going to put in an appearance?' Teresa shifted uncomfortably, 'It was due last week- the lazy little devil.'

'Not it Teresa, He, the son and heir we've all been waiting for, eh father?' Zil spoke with confidence.

'Yes indeed' replied Basil, 'despite Teresa's non-delivery of the goods as it were, up to now, I'm sure it will be a boy this time. It must be a boy- we need a boy badly. He will be the next vital link in the chain which will fasten us firmly in the future.'

'You have an enviable sense of purpose Sir Basil, all of you have- I admire your resolve.' Said Charles.

'My own sense of purpose hasn't helped me at all Dr. Huxley' Teresa replied while her hand massaged her aching and severely put-upon back, 'I've been a great disappointment as a producer of male infants. Fertile indeed but only it seems for females and that's not good enough in this family.' She looked reproachfully at Zil and Basil who both turned away. Neither man made any attempt to reassure her. Charles, surprised at their public callousness was moved, probably by three martinis, to enter into the discussion. 'Teresa, having girl babies is not your fault, the male cell carries the sex factor- it is the man who is responsible for the sex of the child.' It was Basil this time who threw him a disapproving glance.

'Oh I know that,' replied Teresa lightly, 'but I'm afraid it's not so in this house. We're just normally old-fashioned British people. No matter what science tells us, everything, including the non-production of a male heir is always the woman's fault.'

'This has been a rather long pregnancy.' Zil told the table pompously 'my wife seems a little overwrought.' Solicitously he patted Teresa's hand and continued, 'Now don't be silly Teresa, no one has ever blamed you.'

'Then why do I feel guilty? Could it be that you two constantly make me feel guilty, blame or not?'

'Boy babies, girl babies, what's the difference,' broke in Elizabeth, 'they all look alike to me and anyways they are always nasty, red, squalling things. I never had any time for babies- too busy with my stage and film work.'

Chapter Five

'Lucky really that my first and only was a boy,' said Clarissa 'otherwise I would have been condemned to the same fate of mass production as poor Teresa.'

Cook reappeared in time to interrupt what seemed to be an old dispute. She removed the soup plates and replaced them with her masterpiece, the tinned salmon, artistically decorated with slices of tinned beetroot which completely obliterated the contrasting green of the lone lettuce leaf with a poisonous red puddle. The vicar enlivened the eating of this dreadful appetizer with the story of how he had given up smoking, twenty years before. It was a long story, starting with the vicar aged fifteen, seduced by the delinquent companions to take up the evil habit, continued with his additions to twenty-five sticks of the vile weed everyday for almost thirty years. It was at this point that Teresa took her fork and eyeing Clarissa made as if to disembowel herself. Clarissa took it from her and whispered, 'Almost finished now my dear- remain calm.'

The vicar deep into his tale fortunately did not notice the gesture. The story went on to a detailed description of the poor addict cutting down to half a pack a day, continued with the failure of this ruse and reached its climax with the resounding words, 'I said to my dear wife, my late wife Hermione, Hermione I said, I will stop this filthy habit today. With the help of the good Lord I will cast out the devil who has tempted me for so long- I will never touch another one of those revolting cigarettes. And for that moment on- it was the 23rd of the May 1976- and of course with the help of a great many prayers, I never smoked again. It was the gift of the good Lord which gave me the strength of mind to cast out temptation. Anyone could have done it'. He looked proudly around the table.

'Well done!' Said Charles since no one else had the courage or the inclination to speak. It was evident that the story had not been told here for the first time. The vicar now attacked his tinned salmon with gusto while Basil poured an indifferent red wine into their glasses assuring them all that there would be something very special with the birthday cake. Charles, indeed, the entire company having cleaned their plates politely awaited the next course of this grisly meal with trepidation. Clarissa in the meantime whispered to Charles, 'It's the lack of money you see- every last penny goes to the hall, and with four children there's usually not much left for the luxuries.' Like edible food though Charles. The company were right to be apprehensive. After the grey and greasy mutton served with soggy Brussels sprouts and soggier mashed potatoes had been forced down, sighs, not of repletion but of relief were heard. It was time for the birthday cake, which surely could not be worse than anything that had gone before. Steve left the table and soon reappeared carrying a large cake alight with many candles. Elizabeth clapped her hands, 'Oh how lovely- I want to blow out the candles- I bet I can do it even though there are so many.' Teresa laughed, 'You may be able to do it Gran, but you're not allowed to do it- it's not your birthday- it's Clarissa's.'

'Of course- how silly of me I quite forgot.' Elizabeth waved her fan, 'I no longer have birthdays, do I, they're so terribly ageing. Clarissa dear you may have this birthday, I don't mind a bit. I do believe you are looking a mite older today- so sad- you must do as I do, have no more of the nasty things. But the candles are so pretty- couldn't I blow out one or two?'

'No my angel,' said Steve, 'be a good girl now and you may have a piece of cake before bed.'

'I'm no angel,' said Mae West archly 'when a girl goes bad men go after her.'

'Isn't she marvelous,' Clarissa said, 'I swear she's a reincarnation of the original. She's more like Mae every day. Watch now dear, I'm going to blow out the candles and make a wish.' Clarissa blew and the candles, to the last flickering one, expired.

'Well done mother, what did you wish?' asked Zil.

'The same wish I always wish- to live forever- a wish that can't possibly come true- or can it?' She looked at Charles who smiled at her, 'The candles really did go out Clarissa.' 'So they did.' Then Basil, like a magician producing a rabbit from a hat, held aloft a bottle of Chateau Yquem. 'For you my dear Clarissa. There are still a few bottles of this incomparable wine remaining in the cellar, to be opened on special occasions only of course.' He poured the golden liquid into the beautiful Georgian glasses waiting on the sideboard.

Clarissa began to cut the cake and placed pieces on plates which were passed around together with the wine. A toast was drunk to Clarissa on her birthday after which to Teresa's horror the vicar took a deep breath, exactly as before one of his more tedious sermons and began, 'Dr. Huxley since you are here perhaps you would be so good as to tell me something. It's not often that we have a medical expert amongst us and I dare to hope that you will not make it amiss if I ask for your advice. Unfortunately my liver is not what it used to be. Often I experience a stabbing pain just here-' Canon Moffitt pointed to the middle of his rather pendulous stomach. Basil broke in hastily before the symptoms became too authentic and/or disgusting- the vicar had never been afraid to reveal all of his most intimate medical secrets.

'Dr. Huxley is not a doctor of medicine Vicar, he merely has a Phd. Which carries the title of Doctor- not an unusual degree in the

States I gather, in fact rather common- but the nature of the discipline in which he achieved this honour is still a mystery. Perhaps you could finally enlighten us Dr. Huxley?'

'What a good idea Basil.' Clarissa turned to Charles. 'If you've finished your cake Hux, why don't you set up your projector now. I'm sure Basil will help you. Let's satisfy the curiosity which has been consuming him for days.'

Charles swallowed the last dry piece of cake coated with a pink, sickly-sweet icing (Mrs. Payne was obviously a graduate of the same culinary school as Cook) and went to fetch his equipment. He retuned with a screen and a projector.

'Let me help you Dr. Huxley. We are about to be entertained with something called slides are we not? How delightful.' 'Basil- no sarcasm please- its my birthday- remember our rule.'

'Yes dear. Of course dear. Let me help you Dr. Huxley- how about setting up here under the watchful eyes of the first baronet. He is the idealist who built the Hall you know. Look at him- a remarkable face, a man of vision if ever there was one. Fortunately he was long gone and did not live to see the hall after Basil the Profligate, as we call him, allowed the whole estate to go to the dogs. Irresponsible bounder. The damage he inflicted was almost irreparable. But I dare say he would be reasonably satisfied with matters as they stand now.'

'More than satisfied I'm sure. The Hall is a magnificent structure Sir Basil- I'm most impressed with your restorations- you can be very proud.'

'Enough flattery Hux- Basil will be impossible to live with after such accolades.' Clarissa held out her glass, 'more wine please Basil- it's delicious- it really is the nectar of the God's.' Charles agreed, it not only warmed the heart but thrust the recent repulsive meal into oblivion where it belonged. Elizabeth repeatedly waving her fan joined them. 'Basil dear, where is my portrait- it should be up there with the others- I don't see it.' Basil pointed, 'There it is Mother- where are your spectacles, you would see better if you would wear them you know. That is your portrait- up there.'

'Spectacles?' I don't need spectacles- I've never worn them. Nasty unfeminine things, make a woman look too efficient. Men don't like that- just ask me- I know.'

'Of course mother dear...'

'Don't interrupt me Basil. As I was saying that portrait does not depict my likeness. Where is my picture hat? Where is my parasol, my fan? I guarantee thousands of portraits were painted of me. You must remember that I am more famous than Einstein or Churchill, or even

27

Picasso. That's quite something isn't it Dr. Huxley? Basil- I insist that my portrait be hung there with the others, with those of our many illustrious ancestors.'

'Yes mother- I'll see to it tomorrow. Steve- I think the time has come for bed...'

'I'm not going to bed- you can't make me. I want to see the pictures too. That's what you're going to do isn't it? You can't fool me- you can fool around with me but you can't fool me.' The vicar blushed- Basil quickly agreed. 'Alright, Mother alright, you may stay to see the pictures but then bed- promise?'

'Of course my dear boy- I'm a reasonable kind of girl, very reasonable- ask anyone.'

The men arranged the chairs in front of the screen and Charles prepared the projector. The vicar took the best seat as a matter of course. Teresa reluctantly sat down again after a brief walk around the table trying to mitigate the discomforts bestowed upon her by an overdue, and very large baby, as well as the regurgitation heartburn occasioned by Cook. Zil and Basil exchanged condescending glances took their seats- slides for God's sake and doubtless boring- but it was after all Clarissa's birthday and on this special day she could be indulged.

CHAPTER SIX

Clarissa, twisted a handkerchief nervously in her hands and began.

'First of all I must tell you all that Dr. Huxley is a specialist- you were right Basil- he is a specialist in something called cryonics.' Blank looks greeted this extraordinary revelation.

'None of you seem to know what that is- well the word comes from the Greek 'Cyro' meaning icy cold. Cryonics is a relatively new science- it deals with the freezing of human bodies for their future resurrection. Dr. Huxley is an expert in that field- a Cryonicist. He is here too…'

'My God Clarissa you're not…' Basil's had assumed a colour indicative of an imminent outburst of fury. '…you're not involved with such…quackery…such utter rubbish.' 'Oh yes I am Basil, and please do calm down. It's my birthday remember- no scenes.' Basil, his breathing heavy with repressed rage, mopped his forehead in lieu of exploding.

'When I die,' said Clarissa, 'I will not be buried, I will not be cremated- I will be frozen. At some time in the future I will be thawed out and cured of whatever it is that killed me.' A stunned silence reigned for one moment followed by Basil bursting into peals of noisy laughter.

'This is a joke of some kind is it not my dear?' 'Certainly not Basil- I meant every word.' 'My dear Clarissa if that is really so I believe you have finally lost your mind. What you propose is balderdash. This is freezing and thawing and so on is simply not possible.'

'Yes it is- Hux will tell you how it works. But that's not all Basil,' Clarissa was delighting in the furore she was causing, 'in the future when I'm thawed out…' Basil did not let her finish, he laughed again, 'You sound like a fish finger…' Clarissa unperturbed continued, 'When they thaw me out they will have discovered the secret of eternal youth. I will not only be cured of my diseases but I will be completely rejuvenated. Of course after that I will live forever.'

'it won't work Clarissa, it's insane.' Charles who had been trying to speak was interrupted again by a very agitated Zil, 'It's Gran all over again- the birthday cake, the blowing out of the candles; all those years ago it tipped the balance of Gran's mind and now the same ritual has tipped, in fact I'd have to say, completely unhinged, Mother's mind as well. I agree with Father- it's insane. Tell me why, Mother dear why? For heaven sake you're still so young- you can't already be thinking of death.'

'Zil I'm not the only one thinking in those terms. Today everyone in the whole world seems to be obsessed with death and the myriad ways of avoiding it. Just look at the booming health industry, the thousands of vitamins and pills most people are consuming in order to avoid high cholesterol levels, osteoporosis, cancer, senility, or death in any shape or form- as well as all those other evil, life threatening phenomena which lie in wait for us all. I'm merely being sensible- I'm planning ahead.' Charles decided to remain silent- Clarissa knew better than he how to handle her family. His turn would come.

'Don't upset yourself Zil' said Basil, 'I recognise this aberration, it's another of Clarissa's fads. Do you remember the antique clock collecting, that craze that suddenly obsessed her?' 'I do indeed. She was endlessly out raiding antique shops- I remember it became a mania and we could do nothing to dissuade her. It was a distressing time for us all- made worse when she found that wizened old retired watchmaker and put him up here in one of the attics. You won't have forgotten how he drove us all made.' Basil nodded then looked significantly at Charles, 'He may have been old and wizened but he was an expert- and expert and a specialist- in antique clocks.'

'He certainly knew what he was about- eventually he had every last clock working; I remember the ticking the endless ticking. I've never been made more aware of time passing, it was harrowing- extremely harrowing to be reminded of the shortness of time, of the shortness of life.'

'Never mind the ticking Zil,' said Teresa heatedly 'what about the striking –bing bong, bing bong, or ting-a-ling-a-ling all night long. I didn't sleep for months- it was worse than a new baby.'

'Thank God she finally got over it.'

'Thank God indeed,' said Basil 'when I think of the expense!' He cast his eyes to heaven. 'But it only come to a halt when the clockmaker finally dropped dead. Now this expert...' the glance he threw Charles was calculated to annihilate, '...this expert, this specialist, is much younger- he may last much longer.' Clarissa took charge. 'Oh do shut up you too. Hux, what you have just witnessed is a barbaric English habit, speaking about people who are right before ones eyes as though they are not there at all, as though they are perhaps on Mars. No one can have better manners than the English when they wish to be nice, wish to impress or equally, such appalling manners when it suits them to be rude. Please ignore their discourtesy, they are experts of a kind too. I must admit it's true about the clocks. My poor, poor clocks they were so wonderful, they were living beings of me, they had movement, they had life, yet the clocks here were allowed to die. At least Basil still winds the few remaining at the Gate House but there are so many, many more. I should never have countenanced their murder. I must find another watchmaker and get all the ones here at the Hall going again.' Basil and Zil cried in unison, 'Mother please...Clarissa please...'

'Well, look at that Hux, they've noticed me, they do see that I actually exist. They are even somewhat subservient. That's nice. Do you think Basil and Zil that you could persevere with that line while Hux improves your ignorant minds and reveals the truth about cryonics?'

Basil and Zil took their seats. In the civilized way the English have, Cannon Moffitt, Steve and even Elizabeth had, during these heated exchanges looked away politely, pretended not to hear a thing, made as if they were not there at all. When Charles began to speak they returned from wherever they had been and gave him their full attention.

'I can understand that cryonics is a rather overwhelming, even shocking concept but it is happening and happening now. What Clarissa has just explained to you, is possible. There are many cryogenic societies in the States who are doing it every day, my own company amongst them.'

'You mean...you really do mean that you freeze a person after death?' asked Zil, 'We don't call it death, we call it 'suspension'.' Basil broke in, 'I do not doubt for one minute Dr. Huxley, that you and many others are doing this, crazy as it sounds- freezing dead people; many such excesses are perpetrated in America. The question is will it work? I say it will not. The revival of a frozen body is simply not possible; look at that man they recently dug out of a glacier in Austria. He was frozen solid and well preserved but there was no way they could defrost him. Life was extinct. The theory won't wash Dr. Huxley; I repeat, it's quite definitely impossible.' 'Not possible now perhaps Sir Basil- but possible in the future. We are as optimistic about future scientific resurrection as Leonardo da Vinci was about man's ability to fly. I agree that science of cryonics may be in its infancy but we are learning all the time. Problems are being solved every day.'

'Let Hux explain it to you in detail Basil, you'll see it's quite fascinating. I believe in it without reservation. I am going to be suspended. 'Suspended'- how much cleaner a word that is than 'death.' It carries such possibilities, endless possibilities, while death is so- well- so terminal.' A distressed Teresa said, 'I think it's a horrible idea Clarissa- disgusting- totally against nature. You can't seriously be thinking of such a ghastly, unnatural way to leave this earth.' Canon Moffitt cleared his throat, which, on hearing Charles' story, had suddenly seized up. 'I must agree with Teresa, such a process is against nature. There's nothing in the bible about such unnatural practices, it's simply not done.' Clarissa ignored the vicar's platitudes.

'Are you going to let them bury you Teresa, bury you in the earth to rot, to be consumed by worms? Imagine the worms all slimy, wriggling in and out of your eyes sockets. If that is nature I'm against it. Or perhaps you will let them cremate you, burn you to a crisp- nothing left of you but a heap of ashes, your precious molecules reduces to thin, grey smoke.' 'Stop it Clarissa- you're making me ill…' Teresa clutched at her stomach and Zil's hand, 'Mother- please remember her condition….' Zil patted Teresa's hands. Clarissa appeared to relent. 'I'm so sorry Teresa, I forgot that you are in the reproductive, the life-giving phase at the moment. You've a long way to go before you have to face the fact of your imminent dissolution.'

'That's quite enough Clarissa, leave the explanations to Dr. Huxley.' Basil turned to Charles, 'I see my wife is quite determined. Will you let us in on the secret of indefinite survival Dr. Huxley. How is the trick done?' Charles turned on the projector and showed the relevant slides as he spoke.

'As soon as a human body is legally dead a careful freezing process must be set in motion. For living cells to be frozen without catastrophic damage being caused by the formation of ice crystals, the cells must be perfused with a cryoprotective agent- in effect- an anti-freeze.' Basil announced scornfully, 'Really Dr. Huxley- first a fish finger, now a motor car.' Charles ignored him and continued, 'this liquid prevents the water in the cell membranes from crystalizing and thus doing irreparable harm. Therefore the first step is to drain the body of blood and perfuse it with the special chemicals.'

'I've never heard of anything more frightful' cried Teresa 'Zil- I think I'm going to be sick.'

'No you're not darling, you are in the last month of your pregnancy, not in the first. But if you'd like to you could go upstairs and lie down.'

'No…no I don't think so- I'll be alright.' Teresa was as fascinated as the rest of the company by the incredible tales Charles was telling. No one wanted to miss a thing. 'After that,' continued Charles 'the body is put into a Dacron-wool sleeping bag, which stays, soft and pliable at the very low temperature required. It is then introduced into a stainless steel capsulate which looks and acts like a giant thermos flask- just like the one you see there.'

'He indicated the screen on which indeed a picture of a container with the appearance of a huge silver thermos flask was projected. He went on. 'Liquid nitrogen is introduced into the capsule and there we are- the deep frozen body suspended in that medium, ready to be stored at minus 196 degrees centigrade or 310 degrees below zero- that is Fahrenheit. At those temperatures a body will virtually keep forever. It would take eons to wear it out. All that remains to do is to keep the liquid nitrogen topped up.'

'Very well, I accept the freezing premise,' Basil agreed. 'There's the body, frozen solid like a lump of meat- I have no problem with that process crazy as it may sound. But the thawing, the defrosting- how do you do that without damage to the body? You can't just hurl it into the sink like a leg of lamb can you?'

'I must admit, Sir Basil, that is where our main problem lies. The freezing process is relatively easy as you just saw for yourselves. However the thawing process without damage to the vital tissues, is at this moment extremely difficult. But we are learning; we are constantly experimenting with living tissue and coming up with some very interesting results. We are not going to give up on it merely because the process is difficult. You must remember that blood, eyes, by which I mean corneas, not forgetting sperm- human and animal- are already being successfully frozen and subsequently successfully thawed, And that is just the beginning. No- we're not giving up, not by a long chalk.' Basil grinned sardonically, 'Dr. Huxley you will need a very long piece of chalk indeed to facilitate your thawing process. Despite your praiseworthy enthusiasm I think your chances of success are slimmer than surviving a mid-air collision.'

Charles, nettled now, replied, 'The choice, Sir Basil is entirely yours. Traditional interment guarantees oblivion; freezing at least offers the possibility of revival and thus at some future date, survival.

'I think the whole idea is monstrous.' Said Teresa. 'It defies every law of God and nature, particularly the law of God. It is wrong.'

'I agree- it is very wrong,' echoed the vicar, clearly out of his depth.

'Do God's laws preclude progress?' Asked Clarissa. 'Many disasters have been perpetrated in the name of progress mother. Teresa is right- freezing, suspension, all that nonsense is not a Christian way to behave.'

'Goodness you are being pompous Zil darling. What on earth is unchristian about choosing my own method of disposing of my body- my own body Zil. I'm not hurting anyone else.' 'You're hurting Teresa- she's upset.' Teresa echoed, 'Certainly I'm upset; when I think of those poor, unnaturally frozen corpses suspended in those inanimate thermos flasks I wonder what happens to their souls. Tell me that if you can Dr. Huxley.'

33

'I imagine that those who elect to be suspended have no firm belief in the life of the soul after the death of the body. The soul for them is the body. When the body is revived so is the soul.'

Elizabeth sleepily waving her fan began to sing, 'Now I lay me down to sleep I pray the Lord my soul to keep. If I should die before I wake I pray the Lord my soul to take.'

'A lovely song Mother, and beautifully sung. Off to bed you go now- you promised.'

Steve and Elizabeth rose to go, Elizabeth reluctantly. She stopped at Clarissa's side, 'Don't let them talk you out of it my dear- if I wasn't immortal I'd have a shot at that suspension business myself. Fortunately I do not need artificial methods of resuscitation after death. I am alive now and I will live forever.' 'What a lucky girl you are Mother' said Basil 'to be so completely convinced of your immortality.'

'Come along now Angel' Steve took her by the arm and led her towards the door. 'I'm no angel...' And Mae West waved her fan in a sweeping gesture of farewell.

CHAPTER SEVEN

'Well now' said Basil briskly 'if that's all you have to tell us Dr. Huxley I think we might all go to bed.' Clarissa said, 'There's more Basil, much more. Perhaps a nightcap for everyone while Hux continues?' The vicar's gnome-like face brightened immediately, 'An excellent idea- a small whisky on the rocks Sir Basil would just hit the spot.' Basil rolled his eyes, 'Must we Clarissa?'

'We must. It's my birthday. I'll join the vicar.'

'Anyone else?' asked Basil.

'Why not, one for me too please Sir Basil.' Said Charles, grateful for at least a small diversion.

Zil looked meaningfully at Teresa.

'My dear I do think we'd better make tracks… it's late and in your condition…'

'I won't be interrupted in my train of though Zil,' said Teresa 'this matter is far too important. Clarissa must be brought back from the brink on which she is teetering, be brought back to sanity.'

'Teresa my dear- I'm not that far gone.'

'But Clarissa I cannot understand how you can entertain the idea of freezing your body instead of giving it a proper Christian burial. It's blasphemy that's what it is.'

'It's blasphemy that's what it is- I couldn't have said it better myself,' echoed the vicar again, accepting the glass that Basil offered. Teresa in full flight now continued, 'Most people believe in God and God's will, and God's will does not include so called suspension.' The vicar too busy imbibing echoed Teresa once more merely nodded his grey curls in agreement.

'I doubt that most people believe in God these days Teresa.' Charles was not willing to give in to Teresa's condition. 'The percentage of non-believers is larger than you think. After all if so many people had complete confidence in God they would not try to cheat death in as many ways as they do. Clarissa has already mentioned the health food industry; I include fashionable diets, working out, exercising, rejuvenating drugs and all the hundreds of ways that exist for torturing the body, teasing it into shape, tempting it to remain healthy forever. Complete confidence in God's will means they would live normal lives and accept that their turn to die was decreed by a higher authority and would happen to them no matter what they did to prevent it.'

'Some of us believe that God needs a helping hand every now and again.' Basil's derision infuriated Teresa.

'Basil- how could you…you're just as bad as the others.' 'I think we must face the facts.' Said Charles soothingly, in an attempt to calm the protagonists, 'we live in a century which is seriously concerning itself with the prolonging of life. Science, in the past, has worked miracles and we are all living longer than ever before. Now we are on the threshold of even greater discoveries.' Zil would not be propitiated. He replied heatedly, 'And because he is living longer man has become correspondingly more arrogant- he is attempting to emulate God.'

'I wouldn't say that Zil. As Clarissa said earlier, it's simply progression.'

'Progress' said Zil scornfully 'I say we are not now and never will be, immortal.'

'That's only your belief- who knows? And even if God exists- is he immortal?'

'You can't say that,' said Teresa 'you must have faith.'

The vicar, his cheeks happily flushed and looking more like a garden gnome than ever, readily agreed.

'Faith- that is what it's all about- having faith in God.' 'I have faith' said Clarissa, 'in Hux and cryonics. Basil you don't really mind do you? You will let me be frozen forever?' 'My dear Clarissa, this mad scheme is perfectly alright with me. If I'm still around and if you are still determined to be suspended, I will undertake to see to it that you are frozen smartly as directed and immediately immersed in your nitrogenous water bed- or is it thermos flask?'

Teresa's voice verged on the hysterical, 'How can you joke about something so gruesome Basil- you'll be punished- you'll all be punished.' Clarissa intervened, 'Some would have it that life itself is a punishment- is perhaps punishment enough.' Basil retorted, 'Now you're the one being gruesome Clarissa. I suspect it will only be Dr. Huxley and his colleagues who need fear punishment. If what the bible tells us is true, that he is a jealous God then he must be watching you all very closely. After all you are poaching on his preserves. If, in the end you are successful with your cryonics, eternity may no longer be His alone.'

'I am quite prepared to take that risk Sir Basil.' 'It's not merely a risk,' said Teresa 'it's more dangerous than that. You are prepared to risk the life of your own soul in exchange for living forever. I will be happy to take my chance with God. I will have eternal life in paradise.' 'As long as you are convinced of that,' said Charles 'then everything is fine for you, problem solved. Others believe in hedging their bets.' Basil refilled his glass and said thoughtfully, 'You know Dr. Huxley I think your chances of being thawed out in Utopia would be marginally better if you sold your soul to the Devil. Another drink anyone?' 'That's very good, Sir Basil. Very funny.' Charles was finally fed up. 'I am not trying to convince you of the marvels of cryonics, nor am I attempting to persuade you to become a suspensee.' Basil suppressed a smile. Clarissa replied angrily, 'That's quite enough Basil. Hux is only doing his best, at the behest actually, so do listen and stop your silly remarks. Sarcasm won't change my mind you know. Go on Hux.' 'I have simply been explaining to you Sir Basil what it is that your wife has elected to do with her body. Moreover my company in California has had so many enquires from Britain that they have sent me over here to open a new branch. Basically that's why I am here.'

'And Clarissa here is your first customer?'

'Yes indeed and not only my first customer. She has also been kind enough to offer to help me set things in motion- to get the ball rolling as it were.'

In the silence following this latest disclosure the vicar held out his empty glass. Automatically Basil refilled it. The vicar took a sip and cleared his throat, 'Scorpions are notoriously hard to kill,' he told his suddenly astonished audience. 'That remarkable publication The Readers Digest, a magazine you would know well Dr. Huxley, related a recent experiment in which a scorpion was frozen in a block of ice. After three weeks it was released, that is to say the ice was melted and what do you think…?'

'The scorpion survived. I know of that experiment,' said Charles, 'as a matter of fact it was done here in England. It proves, as I said before that we are on the threshold of exciting new developments. I can give you another example. Some species of frogs can survive many weeks with over half the total water in their bodies frozen. Some turtles too can freeze without dying. Cryonicists hope eventually to learn the same tricks.'

Basil, his hand to his forehead in the manner of Rodin's thinker, mused softly, 'First customer…' and with that realisation dawned. 'Clarissa' he demanded, serious at last, 'What is this lunatic scheme going to cost?'

Cannon Moffitt, not usually renowned for his tact confounded the company on this auspicious night. He rose from his chair and made his farewells. As is customary in England the relief the others felt was politely hidden beneath expressions of regret at his departure. Clarissa shook his hand, watched as he was seen to the door by Basil and waited for the sky to fall.

CHAPTER EIGHT

Basil returned, rubbing his hands as though, thought Clarissa, about to chop wood, about to wield an axe.

His tone when he spoke did not belie her fears. 'Well done Clarissa, now that we are alone, just the family, not forgetting the architect of this cryonic madness, tell me my dearest how much is that lunatic scheme of his going to cost?'

Charles wondered why it was that Basil about to chastise Clarissa used so many terms of endearment. Perhaps this was yet another esoteric English habit. Clarissa began to twist her handkerchief in her hands again. It was the question she knew was coming and the one she did not wish to answer.

Reluctantly she replied, 'Not very much at all- considering the complicated processes involved in cryonics. I consider that it's really wonderfully inexpensive- a bargain in fact.'

'I bet it costs more than a funeral Mother,' said Zil, 'even if one does choose the plain pine box with the cheap brass handles.'

'And costs much more than a cremation.' Basil said grimly, 'you're right Zil. A burial or a cremation is carried out, paid for and is then over and done with. I fear this scheme of Dr. Huxley's has another and more sinister aspect; that of maintenance, possibly eternal maintenance.'

Before any one of them could respond to Basil's recognition of the real, the expensive and most distressing aspect of cryonics, Teresa clutched her stomach, doubled up (as much as her large bulk would allow) and groaned in pain. 'Oh Zil, quickly- I think it's the baby.'

'Are you sure Teresa, quite sure, we don't want a false alarm.' Teresa gave him a withering glance and said through clenched teeth, 'After the other four I wouldn't know? Really Zil you are impossible. Of course I'm sure. I'm positive.' Another tremor ran through her and she groaned again.

'Oh my God, then we'll have to hurry, the last one only took forty minutes. Father, will you phone Tony, tell him we'll be at the cottage hospital in ten minutes- Darling where's your bag?'

''Just inside near the bedroom door.'

A relived Clarissa went to fetch it. Even a small postponement of the cryonics debate was welcome. Though she knew well that the crunch was imminent. The cost would have to be revealed to Basil in the end. There was no way of hiding the figures; she had twisted on that particular pin long ago, during her correspondence with Charles Huxley. She had faced the fact herself, now she would have to face Basil and his wrath.

Basil returned from the telephone.

'Tony will be at the hospital in a jiffy Teresa- I told him you were in labour and reminded him to keep his fingers crossed. Come along, I'll see you to the car- here's Clarissa with your bag.' Teresa smiled bitterly, 'Keep his fingers crossed- did you hear that Clarissa? Pray for me please- my life won't be worth living if I produce another girl. By the way I'm terribly sorry to be spoiling your birthday party.' Polite to the bitter end thought Charles. Clarissa laughed, 'My Birthday party Teresa, has suffered more than your intervention. Go on now, I'll be thinking of you.'

Supported on one side by Basil and on the other by Zil the unhappy Teresa made her way out to the car.

Clarissa threw herself into a chair. She was tired out. 'There wasn't much of the party left to spoil, was there Hux? You're seeing English life in the raw tonight and no mistake.' Charles said anxiously, 'I do hope I didn't cause Teresa to go into labour.'

'Good God no- she's a week overdue now- she should be grateful. At least we can thank her for postponing Basil's probing questions- unfortunately only till he reappears. Then we must face the music.'

'We?' asked Charles 'surely it would be better if I went to bed and left you and Basil…'

'Hux if you leave me now I will never forgive you. You're not frightened of Basil surely?'

'Of course not- I can handle it.' Charles was not sure of anything any more but was not yet prepared to admit to cowardice.

'But Hux, I truly don't know if I can handle Basil, I'm frightened of him.'

'Clarissa be brave- take the bull by the horns and just tell him straight out the cost of the whole enterprise. You'll find it will be much easier that way.'

'I will be brave Hux I promise. I will say- Basil, freezing me will cost at the most only 75,000 pounds. Not much really and that includes… oh here you are Basil, everything fine with Teresa?'

'Perfectly. Now Dr. Huxley and Clarissa- no more procrastinating- I need answers.' Clarissa yawned and stretched, 'Not tonight Basil I'm too tired and Hux has had a long day what with driving all the way down here and before that the flight across the Atlantic…'

'On the Concorde no doubt, financed by many unwitting frozen suspensees. Nothing very tiring about that luxurious flight.'

'It's still my birthday Basil and there's nothing I would like more at the moment than a cup of tea.' Clarissa's delaying tactics worked. It was agreed that they would repair to the kitchen and make tea. Clarissa filled the kettle and put it on the Aga to boil. Charles looked around the old kitchen and marvelled anew at what the English could and did put up with. An old stained porcelain sink with wooden draining boards, a yellowing refrigerator clearly rescued from the ark and a cold, hard stone floor. 'Almost the original kitchen you know Dr. Huxley,' said Basil proudly 'though we were forced to modernize it a trifle.' Charles wondered just where the modernization had taken place. He was not surprised that meals such as he had been obliged to eat tonight had emerged from this room. Clarissa found a beautiful Doulton teapot and three matching cups in the pantry, warmed the pot and after the water had boiled again poured it over the Earl grey leaves. Charles thought of his mother making tea back home and the sad little teabag dangling in the cup of nearly hot water. Was that why he never drank tea, only coffee?

They all three sat up at the counter on the stools where Nanny fed the children.

'Milk and sugar Hux?' Charles took both. The tea tasted delicious resembling his mother's not one whit. 'Well now,' said Basil purposefully, 'the evening is just beginning. We must stay up until the son and heir is born. The bottle of Dom Perignon is already cooling in the refrigerator.'

'Basil I can't stay up till late, not tonight please- I'm too tired...'

'Drink your tea Clarissa- it will revive you. I must tell you Dr. Huxley that this evening has been a most interesting one, I would even say stimulating. New ideas always fascinate me and yours are indeed new and quite extraordinary. I find the whole idea of cryonics really intriguing. The most intriguing aspect as I was saying before Teresa left us so suddenly- how much, Clarissa my love, how much will this lunatic scheme cost?'

Clarissa looked helplessly at Charles. Charles hesitantly began, 'Well Sir Basil it's a fairly complex business with so many different processes involved...'

'Nevertheless I think I could understand the complexities as long as you don't go too fast for me, ignorant layman that I am. Take your time, take as long as you want Dr. Huxley.' 'The initial coast- the cryocapsule costs about $20,000 includes the liquid nitrogen- a bargain really. You might call it a steal; as a matter of fact so would I.'

'And after that? Then we have the maintenance do we not?'
'Maintenance and of course storage will cost round about $10,000 a year.'

'Of course, and maintenance and storage goes on forever, increasingly no doubt with the cost of living. I must say I admire you Americans. Nothing it seems is impossible in your country. You have finally devised a foolproof way of taking your money with you when you go.'

'Basil…' Clarissa wriggles uncomfortably on her high stool, '…you're not being fair. When more people join the cryonic societies all over the world the costs will go down. Isn't that so Hux.'

'Certainly. Opening the English branch will help a great deal. We are aiming for suspension at the lowest possible prices.'

'I am delighted to hear it- bargain basement freezing.' Said Basil grimly, 'and no money left for the Hall; and meanwhile Clarissa has the honour of being the first and most expensive customer.'

Charles and Clarissa sipped their tea without replying. There was, at this moment nothing left to say. Clarissa had no intention of divulging the further expenses which she had promised to provide for the new branch of the society; not with the sound of Basil's harsh breathing in her ears and his face suffused with rage, looking as though he was about to succumb to a stroke. Tea drinking proceeded in silence.

When the telephone bell pealed loudly Clarissa's heart lifted. Perhaps the longed for boy had been born at last and would become the diversion she badly needed at this moment. Basil lifted the receiver, 'Yes Tony…what happened. Yes…yes…and then…?' His shoulders sagged sharply, '….another girl. And Teresa?....Fine. Thanks anyway Tony…. yes, yes of course- better luck next time.'

CHAPTER NINE

Charles lay in the uncomfortable bed in the yellow room, uncomfortable despite his having been spared the horsehair mattress. He wondered just what it was the present mattress contained; lumps of some unknown substance, which ate into his back no matter which way he turned. The events of the day had left him over stimulated and jumpy not aided by the so-called silence of the countryside, which was deafening. Crickets clicked and frogs croaked. A plover shrieked probably at one of the predatory foxes which still roamed the fields in large numbers, stalking ducks and hares and keening at the moon- the ancient, barbaric tradition of fox hunting notwithstanding. Dogs barked hysterically in the distance and around him the aged Gate House creaked and groaned as though in pain. All these ominous sounds being the direct opposite of the normal, ordinary traffic noises he was used to hearing from his apartment in Pacific Heights in San Francisco, unnerved him. The gloomy hooting of an owl added to his disquiet.

The flight across the Atlantic in the Concorde had been his first and had been a wonderfully exhilarating experience. However as an excitement, in the true meaning of the word, it left the incidents of this afternoon and evening for dead. He lay, sleepless, rigid and unrelaxed wondering if his plans would ever come to fruition. Not if Basil had anything to do with it, so much was certain. Basil's motivations were beginning to emerge; money or the lack of it, seemingly the strongest and most important; sex, big, but secondary. In brief, Hare Bell Hall was a madhouse, the lack of order extreme, all told- a huge muddle. And Clarissa was part of it, and yet apart. She had qualities which he found he admired after all. She was sensitive, she was vivacious, she was admirable in new ways he had not encountered before. English ways.

Footsteps stole quietly past his door. He listened as they crept on up the staircase towards the turret rooms. The footsteps being heavy, were male footsteps, Charles was sure of it and probably Sir Basil's. Age had not withered his virility it seemed. A wave of pity for Clarissa washed over hum. Poor Clarissa to be so blatantly deceived and in her own house too- it was insufferable. He determined at that moment to do all he could for her. He would support her against whatever importunities Basil might devise in order to prevent her from reaching her own objectives. Objectives, which if foiled, would seriously impinge upon the work Charles was here to do, the opening of a branch of the American Cryogenic Society- Immortality Inc. This company was not an insignificant one. Suspensees in the States already numbered over five hundred and the Society so far was breaking even. Here in England, to begin with his best bet was Clarissa Hare Bell, not only for the money she had promised him but for her probable contacts. He hoped she would be able to introduce him to many more potential suspensees; whole families of suspensees, and above all suspensees with money.

Having come all this way Charles was determined to succeed. He climbed out of the bed and made another vital decision- to take a sleeping tablet. He could not afford the tossing and turning, the sleepless night which was imminent. To be fit, to be forceful, to be on the ball was of the essence- who knew what lunacies might occur tomorrow.

Clarissa lay awake in her bed, alone, listening to the familiar sounds of the countryside. The comforting clicking of the crickets and croaking of the frogs, the distant howl of a chicken hunting fox and the hooting of an owl bent on carnage or cohabitation. Noisy and primitive sounds heralding primitive activities- no niceties in nature- somewhat like my own life she mused. The events of the evening had progressed more or less according to her original plan. Basil had been made aware of her primary intentions. The new revelations would wait until he had become accustomed to that first bombshell. At this moment, she knew, he was being consoled by the acquiescent Steve. Pretty little Steve, an innocent and unwitting assistant, helping to keep Basil's rage at bay. Clarissa felt almost grateful for the girl's beneficent ministrations. She had long ago learned to live with Basil's infidelities which occurred periodically and regularly like the seasons of summer and winter. As for Charles, the personality of the man had begun to emerge; he was not quite as spineless as she had assumed. His business acumen had previously shown itself in his letters and following the discussions with the family this evening she did not doubt that he would persist with his venture no matter what the odds, favorable or unfavorable as events tonight unfortunately presaged. Nevertheless she hoped he would make a fine ally in her battle with Basil and The Hall. Clarissa closed her eyes and slept.

In the turret room Basil struggled valiantly to perform. Steve bravely encouraged. To no avail. Sweaty and disconsolate Basil flopped back onto his pillow.

'It's no use Steve. That woman has finally castrated me.'

'Rubbish Bas, - you've simply had a tough day- much too much agro. You'll be fine tomorrow. And don't call Clarissa 'that woman.' She does her best.'

'Right now she's doing her best to neuter me- to undermine my whole life- to destroy my future and the future of the Hall.'

'Look on the bright said Bas- you've still got me.'

Basil stroked the smooth brown shoulders, the long shapely back. He found cold comfort.

Charles awake heavy-headed to find sunlight seeping into the yellow room. A weak English sun but welcome after his restless night. Outside his window the chirping, twittering and singing of multitudes of birds was thunderous. Where was the tranquility of the English countryside he wondered; was there quiet at any time of the day or night. It seemed unlikely. He found the bathroom unoccupied and after a quick shave and bath in lukewarm water, (no shower here) returned to his room and dressed. The smell of frying bacon drifting fragrantly on the air held the promise of food more edible than last night's abomination. He hurried downstairs and found Clarissa in the kitchen at the stove.

'Good morning Hux- did you sleep well?'

'Good morning Clarissa. What delicious smells- I'm absolutely starving.' Tactfully he avoided her question.

'I didn't realise I was hungry until the irresistible scent of the bacon began to make its way upstairs.'

'Sit down there...' Clarissa indicated the table in the bay window set for breakfast, '...and pour yourself a cup of coffee. Then tell me how you like your eggs.'

'Any way you like to make them.' Charles sat down.

'Clarissa enlighten me- I thought the only beverage it was permissible to drink with an English breakfast was that ubiquitous liquid- tea.'

'You're quite right Hux, but I have an idea that you prefer coffee?'

'You are a mind reader Clarissa, or am I just a boringly typical American?'

'Not boring- but definitely American. However I'm going to fry your eggs and to hell with the cholesterol which, I believe strikes terror into all staunch American hearts'. Charles laughed, 'Cholesterol does more than strike terror- cholesterol strikes dead-very dead.'

Clarissa laughed too and said, 'Too bad- let's take a risk this morning.'

Charles felt a moments guilt before dismissing the faint twinge. As Clarissa had said to hell with it. He was very hungry and cheating just this once could not possibly damage his well-preserved arteries and veins. Normally Charles watched his diet with a ferocity only matched by his attention to business. Somehow, he realised today, his resolve had been considerably weakened- perhaps by the amount of alcohol he had consumed last night, perhaps by the atmosphere of the strange Hare Bell milieu. To hell with it he repeated and found it was quite easy to give in. He felt rather like a schoolboy playing truant- delightfully bad.

'I'll have the eggs fried sunny side up please, just like my Mom makes them back home.' Clarissa broke two large eggs into the bacon fat sizzling in the frying pan and popped bread into the toaster.

'There's orange juice in the jug on the table- help yourself Hux. Basil has had his porridge and is out on his daily sting of life-saving jogging around the estate. We are all alone.'

'I call jogging life threatening not life-saving. Exercise must be gentle, not nearly so vigorous as jogging. But tell me Clarissa, how is Sir Basil this morning- is he very angry after last night's disclosures?'

'We've hardly spoken this morning Hux. He is so incredibly disappointed with Teresa's non-production of the son and heir that the setback has reduced him to silence; a silence that will be short-lived I'm sure. I think he is gathering his forces for an assault. He will try to talk me out of the whole business. You need to know that Hux.'

'Clarissa how can he convince you if you are already committed to Immortality Inc.? Will he, besides rhetoric employ cruelty of some kind? Has he ill-treated you in the past?' Charles shot the questions at Clarissa demanding a true answer. After last night he wouldn't put anything past a Basil fired up with lust for the money to restore his precious Hall.

'No Hux not any of that, we get on rather well most of the time although he always does exactly as he pleases, with very little thought for anyone else. You know- The Master of all He Surveys syndrome. He even rather likes me but you may have realised by now that the gentleman prefers blondes.' Charles was so surprised at this matter-of-fact admission that he swallowed his orange juice the wrong way and choked. Clarissa laughed and she put his eggs down. 'Don't take it too much to heart. Here's a slice of warm toast- enjoy your eggs.'

'You know then- about Steve?'

'Oh yes. She's merely the latest in a long, lengthy line of beautiful, long-legged blondes.'

'Clarissa how awful for you, how can you put up with such deplorable behaviour?' Clarissa poured herself a cup of tea and sat down opposite Charles.

'Well Hux, I know it's a rotten state of affairs but I stand it, I'm used to it. Every time he starts an affair with a different girl it still hurts. Not as much as it did at first of course- his infidelities hurt somewhat more then, but with each girl I become more immune- it's rather like vaccination.' Charles shook his head, deeply puzzled, 'and despite such…. such ruthlessness you still give him money for his own purposes- for the Hall?'

'Well it's mine too, more than ever now since the Hall belongs to our son and to his children as well. Perhaps Basil is right- perhaps the Hall itself does mean something; it will ensure the line; something important, something significant will be left behind. Tradition is hard to ignore. But what do you think Hux?'

'I guess tradition means a lot. We don't really understand that sort of thing in the States, we haven't the weight of the years behind us like you do. But we admire tradition and covet it too; unfortunately it's not for sale. However right now I'm delighting in the tradition of the English Breakfast. The bacon and eggs are delicious. And so is the coffee.' This last was a brazen lie.

'Have some more toast and then you must try Hermione's marmalade. I'll join you in some more toast.' Clarissa put more bread in the toaster.

'Hermione- the vicar's dead wife?'

'Hermione isn't dead. She is an incurable alcoholic. The vicar keeps her more or less locked up in the vicarage and gives out to the world that she is dead. That deception is his way of coping with an impossible situation. We all go along with the pretense, it's kinder for them both. She has occasional lucid phases and when she is reasonably normal Hermione makes the best marmalade in England. Try some.' Charles helped himself to marmalade, spread some on his toast and said earnestly, 'Clarissa forgive me but I must say it- it seems to me that your situation here is also an impossible one. Surely your marriage is a farce. Why don't you leave Basil, why didn't you leave him long ago?'

'Leave him for what Hux, where would I go and why? On a day to day basis we get on very well, we're used to each other. I believe the years together are often a cement which sets quite as hard as love- harder sometimes.'

'You are a very remarkable lady Clarissa.'

'But no saint. That's why I wrote to you Hux. Somehow I do feel cheated. I want another chance, another go at life. I haven't done enough or seen enough, I'm greedy I want more than I've had- I want everything I've never had, and more. Perhaps next time around I'll be luckier. Perhaps next time…' Clarissa gave an ironic smile '…perhaps next time I'll find my true love.'

'And you're a romantic as well'

'As well as what?'

"As well as a saint.'

Chapter Nine

'I've always prided myself on my stoicism- I'm beginning to think it's a doubtful virtue- alright for nuns of course.'

'And saints.'

'A saint no more Hux. You've shown me a side of myself I don't much care for. Now I'm determined to fight my saintliness tooth and nail. Only the vicar could possibly object- and Basil. You will help me won't you?'

'Clarissa you are wonderful. I am personally going to see to it that you get your second chance and Basil will not be able to stop us.' Clarissa's success was in direct proportion to the success of his own venture. If Basil was able to convince her not to part with her money then Charles himself would fail. And he had not journeyed so far from home to settle for failure.

'You say Basil has not broached the subject of cryonics or even money this morning?'

'No Hux- he was unnaturally tight lipped over his porridge. Unlike many people I know, he is generally very bright and voluble over breakfast. There is no doubt that his disappointment over the arrival of a baby girl is severe- he was really counting on a son this time. And we must never forger his daily exertions with Steve- and I do not mean merely the jogging. Those other physical exertions...'

Clarissa smiled wryly, '...I happen to know, overtax him to a degree.' 'Enough to reduce him to silence.' Charles poured himself another cup of Clarissa's weak coffee and continued, 'well Clarissa, that could count in our favour. While he is pondering his next move, we must go ahead with ours. Talk to him while he's still unprepared. Then I promise I will back you up to the best of my ability.'

Charles mentally squared his shoulders, buttered another slice of toast and spread it with the best marmalade in England.

CHAPTER TEN

The sun rose higher in the pale sky and continued to give gentle warmth. Last night's cloud's having withered by day to white wisps, eddied in the light breeze but did not affect the sun's warm rays.

Charles and Clarissa were to watch the children's riding lesson. They walked towards the field where this exercise was to take place. Life went on as usual at the Hall despite Teresa's absence.

'I spoke to Teresa this morning- Zil allowed her to take his mobile phone to the hospital…'

'His mobile phone- she does not have one of her own?'

'You must get used to the fact that we are very old- fashioned here Hux. The men still rule.'

'How is she then? Recovering or as disappointed with her new daughter as your son and Sir Basil?'

'She is not disappointed at all- a new baby is a miracle whatever its sex. And this time she is holding out for a proper girl's name. She hopes to get away with 'Emily.''

'Get away with- does she have no say in the matter?'

'Not really- remember Hux- tradition and the men, they alone rule. The girl's names are all old family names- the names of sons and daughters of other past Basils. They must continue on into the future to satisfy Basil and Zil's sense of the order in all things.' Charles shook his head.

'And your name Clarissa- your antecedents, they are not important in their scheme of things?'

'Life's rich tapestry according to the Hare Bells does not have embroidered upon it the name of the Robber Baron from the Midlands who was my father.'

'Your father- what did he do?'

'Made a lot of money. Serious money. The mere thought of which caused Basil to fall passionately in love with me.'

'Robber baron?'

'It's a joke Hux- makers of lots of money are usually seen by the impecunious multitudes as crooks. My father, and his father before him made the latest, most fashionable models of water closets. Surely a very necessary accessory to a comfortable life style wouldn't you agree? Though my father, never completely comfortable in his line of work, called himself a Ceramic Artist when pressed. And despite his efforts he was never able to bridge the gap between himself- the so called labourer, and the aristocracy, his heaps of money notwithstanding. I'm the one who did that. Basil and his family found him difficult, his conversation being necessarily limited. It would never happen like that in America would it Hux?'

'No – in the States money talks. Money speaks all languages- always has done.'

Their walk having taken them along the rhododendron walk, past Old Leaky and now across an open terraced garden behind the Hall, Charles saw below them a long open field bordered by thick briar hedges. They walked on down to a wooden gate and through it into the field. In the far corner Charles saw Nanny with her pram. Beside her were two small girls sitting on the grass watching their sister who sat on a fat grey pony. Daisy the spaniel stood with a stick in his mouth, waiting for the girls to throw it for him. There were poles lying on the ground and further on a series of more poles balanced on squares of wooden, cross shaped bars set in a long, fenced laneway. In the centre of this equipment stood a plump woman in a white jodhpurs and long black boots. On her head she wore a scarf tied under her chin and in her right hand she held a long, wicked-looking whip. This formidably clad person was obviously the riding instructor. As they approached Charles could hear her loud, harsh English voice shouting.

'Now Harry- forward impulsion. Kick him.' Harriet kicked, ineffectually it seemed, as the pony remained standing and then lowered his head to crop the grass, pulling Harriet forward onto his neck.

'Harriet- shorten your reins, you musn't allow him to eat. Get him going over the cavalletis or you'll have to go back to walking over poles.' Harriet shortened her reins and pulled the pony's head up. She brought her legs to a positional almost parallel with the ground in order to administrate two, even harder, kicks. The pony moved forward into the laneway and stopped to look at the first pole, a mere ten inches off the ground. Harriet kicked once more and the pony stepped carefully over the obstruction. 'That won't do' yelled the riding instructor, 'you must go more quickly over the cavelletis. Get him going faster now, get him trotting.'

'He won't trot Mrs. Owen-Jones, I can't make him. He's horrible, he's a beast.' Harriet was red in the face with fury and frustration. Mrs. Owen-Jones too was not long on patience.

'Hang on Harry…' she shouted and raising her right arm marched forwards towards the pony who on catching sight of the raised whip out of the corner of his eye, began a fast trot over the poles. Harriet was caught off balance but at the last moment before actually tumbling off, pulled herself back up with the reins thus tearing at the horses mouth.

'Use your neck strap to hang on Harry- not the reins. You're hurting his mouth.' Her mentor seemed to think that Harriet was deaf. The pony came to the end of the run and Harriet turned him back. 'That was fun,' she said breathless but quite unafraid, 'can I do it again please Mrs. Owen-Jones?'

'Off you go then.' Harriet pulled the pony around and set off again towards the laneway and the cavelletis. This time she leant forward on her horses neck holding onto the neck strap and kicked the pony who trotted obediently and jumped nimbly over the poles.

'Well done Harry-good girl. Now its Henry's turn. Dismount Harry- hop off.'

'No I won't- I want another turn.' Harriet kicked the pony but Mrs. Owen-Jones was too quick for her. She stepped forward, and took hold of the pony's bridle stopping him abruptly. Clarissa thought it a good moment to interrupt. 'Good morning Mrs. Owen-Jones- how are the young riders getting on?' she pushed Charles forward and continued, 'And this is my friend Dr. Huxley.' 'Come to watch the grandchildren have you? They're doing very well, very well indeed. They'll make competent little horsewomen yet'. To underline her statement Mrs. Owen-Jones slapped her right black boot with her whip- hard; the whistle as it descended was distressing. If Charles expected an involuntary cry of pain from her he was disappointed. Only the pony flinched. Clarissa smiled, 'Under your excellent tutelage Mrs. Owen-Jones, how could they fail.'

'Clarissa, Harry won't get off Thunder Cloud, and it's my turn.' Henrietta lobbyed for help.

'I said hop off Harry.' Steely-eyes and implacable Mrs. Own-Jones gazed silently at Harry as she flicked her whip again. Them she shouted, 'Come along Henry, it's your turn.' Harriet hopped off without another word of complaint and Henrietta was given a leg up onto the back of Thunder Cloud. Mrs. Owen-Jones efficiently adjusted the stirrups for the smaller girl. Clarissa whispered to Charles, 'You see Hux, here, it is not the men but Mrs. Owen-Jones who rules.' The lesson began again. Clarissa turned to Nanny. 'Are the girls pleased to have another sister Nanny?'

'Oh yes Lady Hare Bell. The nursery, I call them 'the nursery' there were so many of them- the nursery, on the whole, approves. There's one of course who has far too much to say for her own good.' Harriet pulled a face behind Nanny's back. Clarissa smiled soothingly and called, 'Harry dear- come her and tell us all about it.'

'All about what Clarissa?'

'Your pony for a start. Tell Dr. Huxley...'

'My pony, that one there, the grey, the one Henry is riding because I lend him to her and to Eddie, but he's really mine, is called Thunder Cloud.'

'What a pretty name,' said Charles, did you think of it?'

'No- it was Clarissa. She said that's what Grandfather's face looked like when she bought the pony for me.' 'And what do you think of your new baby sister?'

'We haven't seen her yet. Nanny is taking us this afternoon. I think Daddy hates her already but he's pretending to like her. And he says we must all like her too. Georgie will have to get out of the pram now.' Harriet said this last with grim satisfaction. Having to walk while her sisters one after another rode along in style had always irked her.

'Watch me, watch me Clarissa.' Henrietta was trotting fast over the cavelletis.

'Good for you darling- now do it again.' Under the stern eye of Mrs. Owen-Jones, Henry did it again.

'Hop off now Henry- it's Eddie turn.' Henry did not argue. 'I would love to buy them another pony but Zil is adamant it's too expensive he says and one is enough for the moment,' said Clarissa sadly.

'You see hux, a well trained, foolproof pony is hard to find and not cheap- and yet sharing a pony is so difficult for the girls, they're always arguing and fighting over poor old Thunder Cloud.'

'Oh well- it's better than having no pony at all,' said Charles who privately agreed with Zil now that he too had a finger in the money pie. 'Great name though.'

'I thought so,' said Clarissa. 'It was obvious as soon as I saw Basil's face. And brace yourself Hux, we're in for more of the same. If I did buy them another pony I think I'd have to call it Thunder Clap; but let's not worry about that now, let's not spoil the beautiful day.'

'I'm very impressed with your grandchildren Clarissa; horseback riding as well at such young ages.'

'They must learn whether they like it or not. Fortunately they do like riding. You see it's part of the system and the earlier they learn the better. Because later they must hunt, and to hunt they must be able to jump their horses over very high obstacles and to do that they must be quite fearless.'

'Hunt?'

'Hunt the vile fox. It's a sport in this country you know. How else will they meet and marry suitable boys? I used to hunt- I loved it. I especially loved the Hunt Balls. Very grand affairs they were and lots of fun. I met Basil at one of them. I believe the labour party are threatening to abolish fox hunting; if that happens I cannot imagine how poor little country girls like my granddaughters will ever find husbands.' They made their farewells to Nanny and Mrs. Owen-Jones, waved goodbye to the children and began to walk up to the Gate House.

Charles turned to look back as they made their way up the hill. The scene was idyllic- the small group set as on a stage on the emerald green grass of the wide field, a child trotting fearlessly on a grey pony, and watching her, Nanny in her brown uniform with accessory (pram containing child.) In the middle Mrs. Owen-Jones in her black boots and royal head scarf, the two young children playing innocently alongside, throwing sticks for the lumbering spaniel, unaware of their destiny. Above them stood the brick and stone facade of the Hall overlooking all, in command, powerfully in charge. A bucolic tranquil idyll, thought Charles, but harbouring a primitive, barbaric past and an even more savage future. The Hare Bell family in the iron grip of unrelenting tradition.

CHAPTER ELEVEN

'I will have to face Basil sooner or later- as you advised Hux so perhaps sooner would be better,' said Clarissa as she and Charles walked by the rose garden. Before them the Hall loomed large and coming towards them at a fast trot they saw Basil with Steve beside him. Charles baulked and made to turn back. Head averted he said, 'Clarissa it might be better if I went on ahead- I ought to get to London and I must pack…'

'You can't go until this matter is resolved Hux. Please don't disappoint me now.'

'Just joking,' lied Charles. The sight of Basil, businesslike and jogging forward determinedly, his green track suit clinging to his tall, fit body has allowed a momentary cowardice to triumph over avarice.

'Good morning Sir Basil, Steve…' Charles smiled bravely, 'are you both enjoying your morning exercise?' Steve nodded, slightly breathless. Basil stopped, and hardly short of breath said, 'You two are out early- been watching the children at their riding lesson?'

He turned to Clarissa, 'I suspect Henry will be a far better rider than Harry- she's more in command of her pony. But they are all doing well and it's really a pleasure to watch the tyrannical Mrs. Owen-Jones at work, she doesn't let the little monsters get away with anything, she never gives up. Which reminds me, Dr. Huxley let me show you the outside of the Hall, the façade in daylight, before we continue our talk. Our talk which was unfortunately interrupted by the recalcitrant Teresa last night.'

'Oh Basil, leave poor Teresa alone- the baby girl is not her fault.'

'So everyone says,' Basil was obviously not all that convinced. Clarissa continued, 'She is going to call her Emily.' Basil frowned. 'Emily is a girl's name; we'll have to see about that. Zil and I favour 'Thomasina', a solid, reassuring, Victorian name appearing in the family of the then Sir Basil Hare Bell in the nineties.'

'Basil that's terrible- sounds like a cat.'

'Nonsense, cats are called Fluffy or Muffy.'

'Basil I happen to know that there is a children's book about a cat called Thomasina.'

'No matter- if that is so the child will have to learn to overcome the allusion. You worry too much Clarissa. Leave these important matters to me and Zil.'

'I must go back to supervise Elizabeth's morning toilet,' said Steve tactfully, 'she tends to wear ball gowns in the morning and bathing dresses in the evening. If Mae West could see her she would be turning somersaults in her grave.' She sped off. Basil continued his attack, 'Clarissa why don't you go back to the kitchen and cook something, or go to the sitting room and dust something- leave Dr. Huxley to me.'

'Said the spider to the fly. No Basil I won't leave Hux to your tender mercies. I will accompany you on the tour of the Hall, if that is what you have in mind.' A good try thought Charles but Clarissa was true to her word; she was not about to desert him.

'Dr. Huxley, I wonder if you would tell us something about your family,' said Basil. 'You are now in full possession of some of the most intimate particulars concerning the Hare Bells and we know nothing at all about the Huxley's. I hope you won't take it amiss if I ask, are you married?'

'Divorced, Sir Basil,'- 'Oh dear- I am so sorry to hear that. Are there any children? 'None. I live in San Francisco, in an apartment with my mother.'

'How interesting. And your Mother? I guess- and here I use the word in its true sense not in the usual American idiom- I guess you intend to freeze her too- tell me is my guess correct?'' Lick me all over and then swallow me whole thought Charles, biting back a retort which could seriously compromise his own pecuniary interests.

'Basil that's quite enough. Don't embarrass Hux.' Clarissa came to the rescue.

'And now Dr. Huxley the correspondence with my wife- how did that start?'

'I wrote to him first Basil. I found an article about cryonics in an American magazine, and it mentioned his name and the name of his company- Immortality Inc. and I was so fascinated by it that I...'

'Since when do you read Time magazine Clarissa? We don't take such spurious American trash; though I cannot imagine that any other respectable publication would concern itself with such nonsense.'

'I can't remember where I read it and it really has no bearing on the matter. In the meantime here we are at the Hall. Stop this interrogation Basil and tell Hux more about your wicked ancestors.'

'Why not- I will provide some more intimate details for you Dr. Huxley. I do hope you do not find these revelations boring?'

'Not in the least Sir Basil- we have nothing like this in the States- I mean nothing as old as the Hall...'

'As old and as decrepit you mean. But, as you people say in the States- we like it.'

'Please Basil...'

Chapter Eleven

'The first Hare Bell who found himself with money- which I must tell you came his way as a result of having the right friends in the right places in Queen Elizabeth's time- as you see Dr. Huxley there is nothing new in this world- with his money this shrewd ancestor of mine purchased a large country estate with a rambling post and plaster Manor-House upon it, built at some time in the fifteenth century. The later Hare Bells soon lusted after something more up to-date, grander and more suitable to their new style of living. Thus came into being, Hare Bell Hall, the brick and stone building you see before you, built in the vaguely Italian style favoured by followers of the architect Inigo Jones. The inside of the Hall you already experienced last night. It is a building which unfortunately requires constant up keeping. Roofs leak, stone frets, and wood rots, not to mention wood being forever at the mercy of the furtive gnawing of the dreaded death watch beetle. And I have not even taken into account the cupola which badly needs re-leading.'

'Basil is trying to make me feel guilty Hux.'

'Not at all- I'm sure Dr. Huxley will make the connection. The upkeep of frozen bodies must occasion similar problems.'

'There are no death watch beetles in liquid nitrogen Basil.'

'Red herring Clarissa- to continue with the zoological theme. I am sure Dr. Huxley knows exactly what I mean.'

At that moment they saw an ancient black motorcar making its slow way along the drive. At last it stopped beside them and Canon Moffitt struggled out.

Lengthy Good mornings were said all round and then ensued a conversation which Charles had expected to hear in England but which so far had eluded him. The vicar began.

'A lovely day, Lazy Hare Bell?'

'A lovely day indeed vicar- so warm, quite temperate for October.'

'But the breeze early this morning had quite a bite to it- a foretaste of things to come no doubt.'

'I hope not yet Vicar- we do need the sun so badly at this time of year, don't you agree?'

'We need rain too Clarissa,' corrected Basil, 'the gardens are looking very dry at the moment.'

'Yes, indeed, the rain last night, just a drizzle really freshened things up quite considerably.'

'Oh yes of course, and those cumulus clouds in the east looking rather ominous- perhaps they signify rain?'

'With any luck, the rain, if imminent will confine itself to falling at night. We do need more sun before winter descends upon us in earnest.'

'We must keep an eye on the sky tonight,' said Basil, 'remember the old adage- when the stars being to huddle

The earth will soon become a puddle.'

'Indeed,' said Clarissa,

'Not forgetting- Red sky at night shepherds delight

Red sky in the morning shepherds warning.'

'Indeed, yes indeed.' The vicar came to a halt.

In the ensuing pause Charles remarked, 'Do you get a lot of fog in this district?' He was damned if he was going to be left out of the conversation. Basil and Clarissa and Canon Moffitt all replied at once, 'No.' 'Yes.' 'Some.' Caught out, they were all at a loss for another word. Charles smiled at their discomfort.

'Morning mists perhaps?' He went on, 'And what about hail or maybe even snow?'

Clarissa laughed aloud. She was secretly pleased that under the earnest Brooks Bros. shirt of the very proper Dr. Huxley there lurked a sense of humour.

But enough was enough.

'My dear Vicar...' Clarissa forcefully put an end to the meteorological musings '...what can we do for you this morning?'

'I brought a pot of marmalade for the little mother,' he said and reached into the back seat of his car.

'Here it is Lady Hare Bell, perhaps you would give it to her- with many congratulations of course.'

'Of course vicar- what a lovely present. I am sure Teresa will be delighted. Thank you so much.'

'Well- that's that. I must move on. Mrs. Winterbottom has found me some items for the jumble sale and I promised to collect them today. Good morning to you all.' He climbed back into the car and slowly and sedately drove away.

'While you're here Dr. Huxley,' said Basil 'let me show you the billiard room. We might have a hit before you go.'

'I'd love to see it Sir Basil but I'm afraid I don't play.'

'He's just trying to get you alone,' said Clarissa, 'but let's look at the billiard room by all means.' They moved indoors and after a walk along a dark corridor turned into a room which had no windows. A full size billiard table dominated the chamber which was lit only by the six green shaded lamps above the table. It was a cold, bleak room. As their eyes became accustomed to the gloom, stuffed heads of foxes and stags materialized, nailed to the walls.

Chapter Eleven

Charles imagined he could see a disquieting look of longing for unattainable and distant woodland in the eyes of these pitiful trophys. The goggling eye of large fish framed in wood echoed their longing.

'Do they disturb you Dr. Huxley?' asked Basil waving a hand at the sad remains of the dead animals.

'Because I can assure you that I no longer shoot- these heads were placed on the walls by my great grandfather. The fish, by the way, was a bombastic Victorian purchase. No one in the family ever fished as far as I know. They have all become rather moth-eaten if one looks closely. Perhaps I should get rid of them.' Clarissa agreed and added, 'you must certainly remove the elephant foot umbrella stand Basil. Recently I heard Harry ask her mother a most difficult and unanswerable question as to its manufacture and origins.' Basil signed, 'everything old is becoming redundant. History is being systemically removed and cleansed in order to satisfy the modern environmental fanatics.'

'We must move with the times Basil- we cannot stand still. We must open our closed minds,' said Clarissa meaningfully. 'I must move on too.' Said Basil his ulterior motives by now fully defeated, 'Clarissa will see you out Dr. Huxley- I haven't done my full two miles yet. Got distracted somehow.' He looked balefully at Charles and trotted off.

CHAPTER TWELVE

It was some time later that Clarissa poured tea into two cups, added milk and handed one cup to Basil. They sat at the table in the bay window of the Kitchen of the Gate House. In the distance crouched the Hall, spotty like a leopard, thought Clarissa, and like a leopard, waiting to pounce.

'Cake Basil- it's very good, one of Mrs. Payne's caraway seed cakes...?'

'I loathe caraway seeds as you well know Clarissa, did you perhaps purchase this cake with that in mind?'

'For heaven's sake Basil I forgot your little peccadillo and anyways that's all she had...'

'Never mind the cake- we have far more important matters to discuss. Where, by the way is Dr. Huxley?'

'Steve and Elizabeth are showing him the walled garden and the kitchen garden. I told him we needed to be alone to talk...'

'We certainly do need to talk. Now this freezing business Clarissa- tell me, after a good night's uninterrupted sleep which I hope you enjoyed, tell mw that you've changed your mind; tell me you won't go ahead with it, please.'

'I must Basil- I've given my word.'

'But how can you contemplate becoming seriously involved in such an idiotic project Clarissa- you do know don't you, what it will mean?'

'I know Basil but it won't be so bad- there will be some money left for the Hall, I promise.' Bitterly Basil said, 'Not nearly enough Clarissa- you know that.'

'Basil please try to understand. This is something I want to do- I feel I must do- before it's too late. In the past- all my life in fact, I've always done whatever you wanted. Now I want to do something entirely for myself.'

'What do you mean before it's too late- too late for what pray? We have always been reasonably happy haven't we?'

'Have we Basil? And I notice you qualify our happiness- by using the word 'reasonably.' I feel incomplete somehow. I suppose I want to assert myself at last and I will Basil, despite your eloquence. This time I am determined.' After a short silence Basil said earnestly, 'Clarissa, I fail to understand how you can be taken in by this American, this Charles Huxley. He's a con man a bounder. Don't you realise he is only after your money?' Clarissa laughed, 'I seem to remember my father saying something very similar to me once, a long time ago. I believe it was on the eve of my marriage.'

'That was entirely different...' Basil's eyes shifted, he was suddenly embarrassed.

'Was it? You know Basil Hux can't possibly disappoint me any more than you already have.'

'Oh rot Clarissa. I cannot accept that. You're overdramatizing. We've had a very good life. Now you are about to ruin everything we have built up together.'

'Yes Basil- you've had a marvelous life- attributable to the combined pleasures of my money and the nubile bodies of you numerous girlfriends. But what about me?' Basil lowered his eyes in a semblance of remorse, 'And don't pretend to pangs of conscience you don't feel...'

'Clarissa, you know very well the few girls I've played around with- that's all it was you know- a bit of a game really- they matter not a jot. They have never mattered. Clarissa you must know that, and know that I love you- I have always loved you. There has never been any question of your not coming first in my life- always.'

'My dear Basil your only love is the Hall- it comes first. Continuity, that's your faith, and your religion. Everything else is only secondary. I just happen to be a part of that scenario, the part that finances the continuity.'

Vehemently Basil declared, 'That's not fair Clarissa, no right. I do love you. I may not be very good at showing it but believe me I do love you. You have done so much for me, for all of us. I can't tell you what it means to me- after all what would the Hall be without you?'

'A complete wreck Basil and you know it. I am not going to succumb to your blandishments. I'm afraid you will have to rethink your position because I am certainly going ahead with Hux on this project. I believe in it.'

'And you no longer believe in me. Well I can understand that but you're wrong. Please Clarissa give me another chance, another chance to prove myself.'

'Prove what Basil, after all this time? It's too late I'm afraid.'

'It's not too late- I love you Clarissa, I've always loved you.' Basil's desperation as he saw the Hall slipping away from him, was showing. He went on, 'There's still time- lets start again. I'll get rid of Steve, I promise- I do love you,...' Clarissa began to feel some stirring of pity for Basil only to suppress those stirring severely and immediately by recalling Steve and the one before Steve.

'You only love me for my money,' she said. Basil changed his tune.

'Clarissa what has happened to you? You've become hard. You were different once- more feminine, softer somehow…'

'Oh yes Basil- a soft touch. If I've become hard it's merely survival tactics at work.' Basil put his head in his hands and was silent. Clarissa said, 'Another cup of tea Basil?'

Through the bay window Charles saw Basil and Clarissa at the table, quietly sipping tea. No angry faces, no load shouting, they seemed to be at peace. Clarissa and common sense must have prevailed. Or perhaps it was the drinking of tea. In every crisis, Charles remembered, the English drank tea- an old tradition which apparently had not yet died. A tradition that seemed to have a lot going for it- calming raging tempests, soothing savage breasts. He entered the kitchen. 'Good afternoon Clarissa, Sir Basil…'

'Hello Hux- cup of tea for you?'

'I'd love one.'

'Where did you leave Elizabeth and Steve?'

'Steve has taken Elizabeth upstairs for her nap.'

The water had now boiled again and Clarissa went about the age-old task of preparing tea. Basil rallied, 'I head you will be leaving us tomorrow Dr. Huxley- where will you stay in London?'

'At the Savoy to begin with,' Basil raised his eyebrows, 'And then?'

'Then I will look for an apartment, as well as trying to find headquarters for my company.'

'And I will be going to London to help him.' Clarissa poured tea for Charles and another for herself. She realised that she was about to need it as Basil's face took on a pinker hue.

'Another cup of tea Basil?' Clarissa saw the gaudy danger signal and attempted to head him off.

'No thank you my dear.' Uh, oh, thought Charles here we go. He was correct.

'And how often, Clarissa, do you propose to dash up to London may I ask?'

'As often as Hux needs me.'

'Staying at the Savoy I suppose?'

'Perhaps.'

'Or later on in Dr. Huxley's flat?'

'Perhaps.' The storm broke.

'My dear Clarissa, do I understand you to mean that you will leave me here all alone while you fart about in London with Dr. Huxley?'

'You've got Teresa and Zil, and Steve and Mrs. Jenkins- you won't be alone. I've already explained the situation to Mrs. Jenkins and she's quite happy to come and cook meals for you if Steve is too weary or too worn out by her many commitments and arduous calisthenics to do so.' Clarissa had scored a point there noted Charles.

'Don't be too downhearted Basil. I'm not leaving you- I'm simply spending some of my money the way I want to spend it. And you might as well know it all now Basil,' Clarissa took a deep breath, 'I have decided to donate a mobile van to Immortality Inc. The van will be equipped to handle the preliminary preparations of dead bodies- on an emergency basis of course.'

Basil's face was by now a deep purple and his fury was such that it reduced him, in crisis mode, to demanding, without uttering endearments of any kind, the usual stimulant.

'Give me a cup of tea Clarissa.' Clarissa poured. Before she could continue, Basil, his voice low and threatening went on, 'You intend to donate this…this machine…this unbelievably expensive, I have no doubt whatever, machine…to donate…a machine' he spluttered and ran out of words.

'Do please calm down Basil- you see the van is necessary in order to take over the maintenance of oxygen and nutrients to the brain. The body is first cooled using an ice bath while a heart-ling machine keeps the blood circulating and administers oxygen.' Clarissa handed him a fresh cup of golden liquid.

'A heart-lung machine…' whispered Basil at breaking point. Burning his tongue and let fly with a word Charles thought would normally never have passed the noble lips. Clarissa wisely decided to change the subject. Her face falsely cheerful, she broached an entirely new notion, 'Basil, we must visit Teresa tonight after dinner. I know she's longing to show off her new baby. Has a name been decided upon yet?' Basil rallied a little, 'Teresa has agreed to Geraldine.' Even this concession on Teresa's part did not cheer him.

He looked, thought Charles crushed, yet wary and alert like a dog whose bone is about to be taken from him- a dog who will not surrender his bone without savaging the injudicious thief.

CHAPTER THIRTEEN

Teresa Hare Bell lay in her bed in the Major General Arbuthnot ward- the cheerful two bed maternity ward having been made possible (and cheerful,) by the generous donation of Major General Arbuthnot, and admired her fifth daughter who lay in a bassinet beside her. In the bed opposite Daphne Tilletson suckled her third son. Above her on the wall at which Teresa was forced to gaze unremittingly hung a picture consisting of a mélange of colour photographs of babies who had (presumably) spent their first days in this ward.

Red, wrinkled and almost identical, distinguishable only by pink or blue garments clothing these ugly, still foetus-like, future human beings, they caused the onlooker, in this case Teresa, to despair at the cruel tricks of nature, as well as at the profound knuckle headedness of the person who had thought up the idea and then framed the results.

Daphne had the good fortune to be able to gaze at prints of small children with very large heads gamboling with woolly lambs in fields of clover in which bloomed red, yellow and purple shapes representing unlikely (in this world at least) flowers.

'It's no good Teresa,' said Daphne 'you will have to take sterner measures. There is a way you know, to produce a boy baby,'

'There is? Other than pure chance' Teresa did not sound in the least interested.

'There certainly is and I suggest you acquaint yourself with the medical facts.'

'Medical facts? Daphne I know that each time those cunning little sperms make the dash for the egg the chances remain fifty-fifty no matter what. Better to try witchcraft.'

'That's not true Teresa- there are methods that can be most effective.'

'How do you know all these things Daphne?'

'We've been doing it...'

'Trying for a girl I suppose.'

'Well yes,' admitted Daphne unabashed. Teresa laughed, 'with conspicuous success I see.'

'It will work next time I'm sure. The idea is to correctly identify the fertile period and the day of ovulation.'

'How do you do that?'

'Well...' said Daphne reluctantly 'it's fairly yucky really. I have the book at home- I'll lend it to you.'

'If it's that bad I want no part of it,' said Teresa.

'But you don't really want to produce another girl do you Teresa- after all five has got to be enough. Though I must say I admire the way you cope with Zil's obvious disappointment.'

'I take no notice- if I did I'd be locked up in a funny farm by now. Anyway I assure you there won't be a next time. This is my last hoorah. No more babies for me Daphne. I have put my foot down, mentally at least.' It was Daphne's turn to laugh, 'That's what you think. I can just see old Sir Basil and Zil accepting that ultimatum. I bet they're already planning your next pregnancy.'

'Then they had better start making corresponding plans to marry off five daughters. A thankless and virtually impossible task. I can get out of the next pregnancy, Daphne, by simply reminding them of that small and insignificant detail- the one they keep forgetting. Bad enough with five daughters, but six! No- I think they will see reason this time.'

'Teresa you must have another try. The book tells one the exact time when intercourse produces a boy and when intercourse at another time will produce a girl. It's really quite easy.'

There followed further grisly details, none of which in the least sounded easy to perform and none at all pleasant which caused Teresa to pull a face, 'Intercourse, intercourse- you must be joking Daphne. There will be no more intercourse at Hare Bell Hall from now on and into the foreseeable future. It would have to be rape.'

Teresa looked up and saw two men entering the ward, 'Why- speak of the devil or in this case two devils- look who's here; hello Zil darling, and Basil- nice of you to come.' Basil and Zil bearing flowers kissed Teresa and threw a perfunctory glace into the bassinette beside her bed. Basil went across to Daphne who was replacing her son in his crib.

'Another boy I believe Daphne?' Basil looked enviously at the bundle in her arms. Daphne nodded guiltily. 'Well done,' signed Basil and turned back to his granddaughter. Teresa had taken the baby from the bassinette to show her off. The dark head and retroussé chin were pure Hare Bell.

'Isn't she gorgeous?' Teresa smiled at her baby as Zil and Basil made an effort to dismiss their what-might-have-been thoughts and patted the baby's head. Then sister Anita, head midwife came into the ward and clapped her hands. 'All babies to be back in the night ward in ten minutes. And dry please mother.' Daphne and Teresa dutifully removed dirty nappies (disposable- no one could call the Cottage Hospital backwards- merely environmental unsound) and wrapped their small bundles up in their blankets.

At that moment Clarissa and three little girls ran into the room. Two of them flung themselves onto Teresa.

'Mummy, Mummy, is this the baby?' the two looked eagerly into the crib only Harriet hung back.

'Not another girl' she sighed, raising her eyes to heaven. 'Harry,' said Teresa,' this is not the time to emulate your father or grandfather. You should be on my side.'

'What's emulate,' asked Harriet.

'Emulate means taking the same path, in this case following in the same fatal footsteps as the Hare Bells.'

'What's fatal?' Harriet often succeeded in becoming the centre of attention.

'Destined, doomed, and now behave yourself Harry,' said Clarissa 'or you will be doomed to eating a nursery tea. No MacDonald's for you tonight. And now many congratulations Teresa and well done. This baby is quite beautiful.'

'Thank you Clarissa, only you understand. And are you really going to take your life in your hands- dining at Mac. quicksick?' Basil broke in, 'Why not bring a little joy into the poor deprived lives of these little girls- or lives that soon will be deprived if Clarissa continues with her ludicrous freezing scheme.'

Teresa laughed at his moody face.

''Still sulking Basil?'

'Freezing frenzy I call it,' said Zil 'but give her time I reckon she'll get over it- like the clocks. Don't dwell on any of it Teresa- such obscene thoughts could curdle your milk.'

Sister Anita swept into the ward, clapping her hands again, an activity in which she clearly excelled.

'Babies and visitors out now- at once,' she took both cribs and wheeled them briskly towards the door.

'Time for Mother's rest,' she said, fixing the two mothers with a steely eye that flattened them instantly onto their pillows. To deny Sister Anita's demands was tantamount to insubordination of the worst kind, punishable by long, slow torture- a tongue lashing from Sister Anita's rough tongue. The visitors kissed Teresa one by one and trailed obediently out the door.

Basil threw another log onto the fire in the sitting room of the Gate House. The evening was cold and the fire made the room not only warm but also cosy.

'I gather you will be leaving us tomorrow Dr. Huxley?'

Basil did not sound unhappy to be losing his guest.

'Yes Sir Basil, I'll be driving back to London tomorrow- got to get the ball rolling.'

'You mean get the balls freezing.' Basil smirked at his own wit.

'There will be no freezing yet Sir Basil.' Charles, in the logical, American way, took him seriously.

'You see the first step in the process is to set up an office as the home base- our headquarters. Then we must find a large space such as a warehouse where we will later store the vacuum flasks containing our suspensees. After that we will advertise and hope for a good response.'

'And where does my wife fit into that scenario?' Clarissa to deflect the answer replied quickly, 'I'll be helping to set it all up and to guide Hux through the pitfalls of the English way of life...'

'Pitfalls what pitfalls?'

'The class system, just for a start.'

'There's no such thing Clarissa- unfortunately, and I repeat most unfortunately the so-called class system has all gone- been eliminated by an act of parliament- by the will of people, you know that.'

'All gone? Not really Basil. Think again. In any case I will be able to help Hux with many things which include getting the ball rolling as he put it, under the mobile van...'

'Oh God- the one containing the heart lung machine.'

'Yes Basil- that one. And now its bedtime. We've all had a big day.' Basil ignored her and moved to the drinks cabinet.

'Would you like a small nightcap before retiring Dr. Huxley? I certainly need one.' He opened the cabinet and took out a bottle of Macallan Whisky. Clarissa realised at once that the suggestion was premeditated. It was not for the love of Charles Huxley that Basil was offering him his best malt whisky.

'I'll have one too thank you Basil. Hux one for you? The Macallan is a delicious drink, distilled and bottled in Scotland- the best single malt whisky in the world.'

'After that fantastic testimonial how can I refuse? Yes please, sounds like a great idea.' Basil poured generous measures into three glasses. Clarissa continued, 'Now come clean Bail- what do you want from Hux?' Basil looked injured.

'Nothing in particular- I simply wish to know more about your scheme, your cryonics Dr. Huxley. I need to get it straight in my own mind.' Clarissa frowned. Basil turned on her, 'And what is wrong with that Clarissa- I do wish you would go to bed and leave me alone with Dr. Huxley.'

'That is exactly what I will not do. I would not dream of leaving Hux to your tender mercies.' A relieved Charles said quickly, 'What would you like to know Sir Basil- I am only too happy to answer any questions you may have, I would really like to set your mind at rest.'

'You may find that more difficult than you suppose, Dr. Huxley,' said Basil throwing down he glove. Charles, on his mettle, listened attentively. Basil continued, 'On reflection, I find the philosophy behind the thesis of cryonic preservation most puzzling. It seems to me that the freezing of a human body for future reincarnation is the demonstration of monstrous egomania- you would have to agree with that would you not?'

'No, Sir Basil, I would not agree,' replied Charles bravely. 'Self-preservation is a natural instinct- we all have it. Cryonic preservation is simply an extension of that basic human instinct. I do not see it as self-serving or maniacal in any way at all.' 'But you must admit Dr. Huxley, that the whole concept is ego driven, is utterly selfish.'

'Not at all- we are pushing the horizons of science further than ever before. These efforts will doubtless benefit the whole of mankind in the future. A praiseworthy endeavor surely?'

'I think not Dr. Huxley. To get back to my original premise, the selfishness of your science is obvious. For instance, that you Clarissa, want to live forever- I mean to say it's ridiculous. What do you have to offer the world after you are defrosted?'

'Basil that is unkind. I have just as much right to be preserved for the future as anyone else. I simply do not want to die- not permanently.'

'You mean you are afraid to die.' Said Basil.

'I suppose I am- but that is not a crime Basil.'

'It is not a crime but it is very silly. I can prove to you that your fear is irrational. In the first century BC Lucretius gave us this thought- the eternity before your birth is identical to the eternity after your death. You do not find it fearful to consider the eternity that preceded your birth- therefore why fear death and its similar eternity?'

'I have thought about those words too.' Said Charles immediately, 'and considered them deeply. At first I believed in that view of life and death. But then I came across the American philosopher Thomas Nagle who sees a different picture. He maintains that the two eternities are dissimilar. Death deprives a person of life- birth does not. We fear death because it means the losing of life.'

'I agree with him,' said Clarissa, 'And having lived once, I want to live again- I want to live more and better next time around and I want to live forever.'

'But you have no right,' said Basil, 'you are unimportant in the scheme of things.' Untroubled, Clarissa sipped her drink.

'That may be your opinion Basil but you have not convinced me of my worthlessness. In any case I do have more right than most...' she smiled, '...I have the money.'

'So that is the secret of life- money. Not that I ever doubted that premise. I am surprised Clarissa that your thought processes touch bottom so quickly- you have become sadly shallow.' Basil swallowed the last of his whisky. 'I think I will retire. I can see that there's no convincing either of you philistines to abandon your grotesque, biologically insane machinations. Good night.' As Basil made for the door Charles forced himself to say, 'Before you go Sir Basil I must tell you how much I have enjoyed my stay with you.' He meant it. The insight he had received into the English way of life and English manners were invaluable- as well as entertaining.

'I am delighted that you have enjoyed yourself Dr. Huxley. Do come again when you are able to take time off from your onerous duties at the freezer.'

'Goodnight Basil,' Clarissa was laughing. When he had gone she turned to Charles, 'Basil has finally accepted that I will not budge. It remains to be seen what further measures he will take to dissuade me from my purpose and so preserve the Hall in the manner to which it has, over the many years, become accustomed. I wouldn't put anything past him now- he's a cunning old fox when roused. Meanwhile I intend to do everything possible to preserve my own body, be it egomaniacal or not. Another small whisky Hux?' Gratefully he held out his glass.

In the morning Charles consumed orange juice and bad coffee and soggy toast spread with the best marmalade in England. Then he packed the rental car with all his equipment and his clever American luggage and set off for London with Clarissa's travelling instructions set out in detail on a piece of paper on the seat beside him. He arrived in the capital in under two hours, making better time than on his trip down to Hare Bell Hall.

He checked into the Savoy Hotel in good shape after driving (inadvertently) only twice around Trafalgar square being in the wrong lane for The Strand at the time. He was finding driving on the wrong side of the road as strange and as peculiar as the two days he had just lived through. But, he reflected, just as he was becoming familiar with driving on the wrong side of the road he felt now that he could easily become used to the peculiarities of England and the English, and even admire them and their eccentricities, given a little more time.

His room overlooked the Thames and a bridge over which the traffic rolled grey and unremittingly, enlivened now and again by a bright red, double decker omnibus. A light rain was falling. The scene was straight out of an English movie thought Charles and lifted the phone. He felt suddenly quite homesick, quite out of place. He had no wish to find himself in an English movie and yet here he certainly was.

'Room service please,' he said and feeling a twinge of guilt ordered from the room service menu- 'An American hamburger with all the trimmings accompanied by French fries and a New York pickle.'

CHAPTER FOURTEEN

Clarissa Hare Bell sat with a towel wrapped around her wet hair, consulting a colour chart rather like the ones produced by house painters for selecting the colour of walls. Clarissa was about to choose a new colour for her hair. Harrods hairdressing salon had a warm, comforting atmosphere for such an important event; full of ladies in flowered smocks, sitting quietly, chatting, smoking, drinking coffee and being simultaneously washed, set and blow dried. There was no pressure here, no tension, there was time to think, time to consider, time to waste.

For several months now Clarissa had been going up to London regularly to help Charles Huxley with his new organisation. It was only last week that she had decided to do something about her hair. Dealing only with the local village hairdressers and being unwilling to trust the pedestrian Tracy with such a serious matter as hair colouring she had been in a quandary. Where to turn for up-to-date information on hair? Teresa being preoccupied with maternity and also in the habit of frequenting the village Tracy had no advice to give her. Clarissa turned to Daphne Tilleston who told her that Harrods, though perhaps not as fashionable as some was as proficient a salon as any other. So here Clarissa sat, sitting in the quandary. What colour should she choose? Black, blonde, brown or red? There were really only four choices with seemingly hundreds of variations upon those four primary hair colourings. Her own original colour Clarissa was forced to admit but only to herself, had been a kind of mousey brown. In the fullness of time it had turned to pepper and salt and then moved relentlessly on to a dismal grey. Much too early really for her age, Clarissa assured herself, so it made sense to change. It had nothing to do with cheating or with vanity- nothing at all. In the past the grey had not seemed to matter since only the village and her family were there to notice but no, being in London so often and with Hux around- well, it would not do. She had let the severe short cut she usually sported- a practical, functional cut-grow out a little and was ready for a new colour and a new style. 'Well, Lady Hare Bell have we made a choice?' The curled and primped young lady who now appeared at her side wore a very short skirt displaying black legs, dumb-bell shaped and entirely unsuitable for the tights encasing them. But she had a kind and reassuring smile.

'What would you advice, Kylie?' Was that her real name or had colonial television caused these strange upheavals in the naming of Children?' Clarissa forced her mind back to the colour chart.

'I thought this tawny colour might suit me- what do you think?'

'That is exactly the colour I would have chosen Lady Hare Bell- youthful without being…well you know..'

'Yes—'tawdry' is I think the word for which you are searching Kylie.' Kylies open mouth and blank eyes indicated that she was not searching for a word at all. The word, a much coarser one had been on the tip of her tongue; however she was a tactful child- a prerequisite of employment at Harrods. But now Clarissa had her decision.

'Well Kylie since you agree-let's do it.'

Some hours later Clarissa emerged looking, she thought most odd. She hardly recognised her reflection in the mirror; the soft new style framing her face and curling delightfully around her ears complimented her rosy complexion and her eyes an even more startling blue. One thing was certain- her image looked if not familiar to herself, at least ten years younger. Why, she asked herself as she hailed a taxi in Brompton Road, did I not do this years ago? More precious time squandered- times she should have used to her advantage. She was reminded of all her clocks at home, ticking the minutes, the hours, the years away.

The taxi was taking her to the headquarters of Immortality Inc. situated in the Kings Road, Chelsea not far from Peter Jones. The four room office space was on the first floor of a building which housed a clothing store on the street level. The store sold leather and metal studded outfits suitable only, Clarissa explained to Hux; for exceptionally thin bikies of any or every gender. Music of the earsplitting variety issued forth onto the street, preventing, with this wall of noise, any unsuitable potential buyers from entering. A discreet brass plaque on the wall at the entrance to the stairs leading up to the first floor declared,

Immortality Inc. U.S.A.
President- Dr. Charles Huxley.
Vice-president- Lady Clarissa Hare Bell.

The four rooms were spacious and contained all the most modern American equipment that Charles Huxley had been able to acquire from the American branch. He was well set up, and contemplating sound proofing. Clarissa stopped the cab in Sloane Square, she wanted to walk a bit, to become accustomed to her new appearance. She walked slowly, swinging her umbrella and looked covertly into shop windows as she passed by. She was pleased with herself; she smiled at her reflections and mourned the lost years. The windows of the health store on the corner caught her attention.

Chapter Fourteen

Amongst many bottles of pills and jars containing odd coloured liquids hung a printed notice. Clarissa read,

No More Guessing- no More Leaving Those Major Life Decisions to Fate- Now You Can Make A Boy Or Girl Baby To Order.

Intrigued she entered. The young girl behind the counter did not look old enough to vote. Her pale unhealthily botched face framed in a pillar box red, long and lanky hair did not inspire confidence. Nor did her ears which were pierced with many small golden rings from one of which depended a silver elephant with cobalt blue eyes and a long, phallic like trunk. The weight, presumably of the elephant caused her head to tilt to one side. She smiled brightly at Clarissa and mouthed the formula, 'How may I help you?' Exposing brownish stained teeth. Did she chew tobacco? Or perhaps vitamin pills? Clarissa said, 'The notice in your window- I'm interested, I'd like to know more about it.'

'Oh sure- we've had lots of enquiries about that. Your first baby?' Clarissa blushed. The girl ploughed on, 'Don't be shy- I know- let me guess- you've had boys and now you want a girl- am I right?'

'No…not really- it's for someone else.'

'They always say that,' said the girl smiling 'There's nothing wrong with it you know. Mind you there have been some complaints- I mean we've had various religious organisations in here bitching- they reckon it's not natural, reckons it's unchristian but for God's sake, I say why not have the sex you want- if you know what I mean.'

Clarissa not knowing whether to feel flattered or whether she was being conned asked,

'Well then- tell me- how is it done?'

'First of all what do you want- a boy or a girl. You see it all depends on the sperms, those speedy little wrigglers. Each one carries a chromosome which determines the sex of the baby. The idea is to get the right sperm to the egg at the right time. Once you know that you're ahead of the game, Now tell me- do you want a boy or a girl?'

'A boy. You see its my…' Clarissa stopped there; she felt as though she was betraying a confidence. '…I mean it's for a friend.'

The girl nodded and the elephant shook his trunk in unison with her red locks.

'We can do that. We've had fantastic results- 100% every time. Here…have some pumpkin seeds- they're roasted. Very good for the digestion.' Clarissa bemused- took one. It tasted delicious. This weird girl seemed to have taken a liking to her and while the encounter seemed wholly out of this world Clarissa stayed. 'There are more things in heaven and earth' she reminded herself and who was she to be skeptical. Perhaps this unlikely apparition really had the answer.

'Did you know...' the girl continued confidentially, 'that whale sperm are exactly the same size as human sperm. Isn't that awesome? Of course that whales have much more sperm then humans, some tons more. And do you know who has the biggest sperm in the animal kingdom?'

'No idea' said Clarissa and took another pumpkin seed. 'It's the honey possum- a small Australian marsupial.'

'How fascinating. But do tell me- how does one make a boy?'

'Well, the idea is to kill off the sperm carrying the female chromosome and that can be done with diets high in salt, as well as with the necessary herbal mixtures.'

'Do you have them here, the mixtures.'

'Sure- I can make one up for you in a few minutes. And you will need the instructions as well' 'Instructions?'

'How to use the mixtures in your every day diet. For instance to make a boy all dairy foods should be strictly avoided. And that is just the beginning.'

'It sounds awfully complicated,' said Clarissa uncertain now that she was doing the right thing.

'If your friend- I think you said friend, wants a boy badly enough I should think she'd do anything to achieve her goal.' The girl seemed to know what she was talking about despite the heavily swinging elephant which Clarissa found increasingly repellant.

'How much is it?' she asked.

'Thirty pounds the lot. And cheap at the price.' Oh well, thought Clarissa I can afford it and who knows it might even work. That is if Teresa herself would ever be interested enough to follow all the complicated directions and to swallow the probably very nasty herbs.

'Alright then- make up the mixture for me. Will it take long?'

'Only ten minutes or so, here...' the girl handed Clarissa the printed sheets.

'These are the directions- you could read them while you wait.' Clarissa looked at her again as she disappeared into the back of the shop. Looked at the childlike face and the horrible hair. So young and already so full of esoteric knowledge- it seemed totally incongruous with her looks- or am I getting old thought Clarissa and applied herself to the directions. They made curious and unpleasantly detailed reading.

The girl soon returned with a small package the size of which did not seem to Clarissa to be worth the asking price. 'The best things come in small parcels,' said the girl shaking her scarlet locks. And she's a mind reader too thought Clarissa as she paid and took her precious parcel. 'Good luck,' said the girl or was she a modern day witch, 'there's one last piece of advice I have for your friend. Tell her the full moon- that's the best time for boys- mind you don't forget.' Definitely a witch, silently said Clarissa.

Clarissa climbed the stairs to the office with a diffidence she had not felt since she was fifteen. Her new youthful look would surprise Hux but what would he think- what would he say? His opinion was beginning to matter to her.

'Hello Hux.' He was sitting at the computer concentrating on spreadsheets. He barley looked up saying, 'Hello Clarissa- we have another suspense. That makes eight, isn't that great?'

Clarissa leant over his shoulder to watch the screen as he worked.

'It certainly is Hux- how did you manage it?' Charles looked up at her and the open-mouthed surprise on his face made Clarissa laugh.

'I...I mean you...you...what have you done to yourself? I hardly recognised you.' He did not wait for her reply and went on, 'You look absolutely stunning!' Clarissa blushed for the second time that day.

CHAPTER FIFTEEN

Basil Hare Bell was dreaming. The dream was terrifyingly real. He found himself in a large, dark, echoing warehouse from the ceiling of which hung life size steel, vacuum flasks. They were swinging eerily back and forth, back and forth, not together but out of sync, moving like shiny ,giant, metal maggots feeding on dead flesh. He knew that inside these futuristic containers were people- naked people, dead people, suspended in freezing, cold, liquid nitrogen. He knew that he was one of these people- he knew too that he was not dead. The liquid washed icily over his head and face and over his whole naked body beginning, he realised with horror, the freezing process. The cold, extreme now, crept under his skin into his viscera into his very bones and he felt his body stiffening in response.

'Stop- I'm not dead- stop, please stop.' He shouted, but his voice was muffled as though he was shouting through layers of cotton wool and to his increasing dread he realised that no one could hear him. He tried again to move his arms, to move his legs to run away from this horror engulfing his whole body but his efforts were futile. To take each breath became a supreme effort and now something quite gruesome was touching his body, was leaning heavily on his chest, trying, he knew to stifle his cries, to stop his breathing, to reduce his body to a frozen hulk.

'Wake up Basil…wake up' said Clarissa shaking him, 'You're dreaming.' Basil struggled to emerge from his private nitrogen bath into light and freedom and soon his struggle was rewarded. He found himself in bed, with Clarissa beside him. On his side of the bed the covers had fallen to the floor and since he slept without pyjamas he was feeling extremely cold. His teeth began, belatedly to chatter.

'Basil if you persist in sleeping in the nude you will eventually catch pneumonia. Did you have a nasty dream?' Basil recovered his doona from the floor and cowered beneath it.

'Nasty? Was I shouting by any chance Clarissa?'

'Not shouting, just groaning and moaning as though you were being tortured. What was happening in your dream?' Basil smiled wryly, he was not about to confess to the new Clarissa.

The new Clarissa- not only younger and surprisingly more attractive than of yore but more energetic, more alive more like the Clarissa he had married long ago. Over the years he had become complacent in the knowledge of her acceptance of his foibles (currently Steve) but the new Clarissa seemed no longer as submissive as before-the new Clarissa was taking charge, and the new Clarissa, he thought bitterly, was taking some getting used to. And not only that, now too there was that American maniac Charles Huxley to reckon with.

'I really don't remember my dream Clarissa,' he lied, 'though I suspect your friend Dr. Huxley was in there somewhere- he's a nightmare incorporated all on his own.'

'Don't be horrid Basil, just because Hux is becoming so successful in his work and after such a short time too. I believe you're jealous.'

'Jealous- of an American? You must be joking Clarissa. And now I'm going for my run. I'll be back in time for breakfast.'

Basil and Steve had reached the bottom field, well out of sight of the house before he reached for her. Their embrace was long and as usual after their run, sweaty. Steve broke away first, 'Not here Basil- I must get back.'

'Rubbish- lets go around one more time. I feel so lively today I could do another half hour at least.' His relief after the terrors of the night was expressing itself in a renewed zest for life.

'Or…he smiled at Steve, a smile perceived as sexy, '… perhaps something a little more strenuous?' Steve was becoming rather tired of hasty, sweaty intercourse with little reward. 'No Basil I really can't. I must get Elizabeth up. She's liable to dress quite outrageously if I'm not there.'

'She does anyway- even when you are there.'

'Little do you know- sometimes she puts on stockings and a hat and absolutely nothing else.'

'Well for a forgetful old lady she certainly throws herself into the part, I will say that for her.' His mother was one more fact of life that Basil preferred as often as possible to forget. The two set off again and soon reached the Gate House.

They found Clarissa in the kitchen making tea. She was wearing a luxurious, filmy, black negligee, almost but not quite transparent. She did not greet the two runners with a smile.

'Good morning Basil, Steve- nice morning for a run. Oh, and Steve, Elizabeth is crashing about upstairs muttering that she can't find her red suspender belt…' Steve feeling herself dismissed said tactfully, 'I'm on my way.' She disappeared as Basil eyed Clarissa's appearance with disapproval.

'You're looking a little too glamorous for the kitchen this morning Clarissa- I haven't seen that outrageous outfit before have I?

'It's just a little something I picked up in London last week- Like it?' At the mention of London Basil frowned.

'You go up to London far too often lately Clarissa. Remember what Tony told you- your blood pressure is up and you must take it easy. All this traveling is bad for you- you'll exhaust yourself.'

'Tony is an alarmist- there's nothing wrong with me. In any case I'm not going to London this week, Hux is coming down here. We must get the books straight. You'll like that won't you Basil?' Basil frowned again.

'You're seeing far too much of that crazy American.' 'Does that bother you Basil?' Basil ignored the question and threw out one of his own.

'Are you still determined to go on with that nonsense of Huxley's- you're not tired of it?' Clarissa shook her head. He went on hopefully, 'or bored perhaps?'

'I most certainly am not bored. The Society is proceeding in leaps and bounds, we never dreamt it would grow so quickly. We have dozens of enquiries every day- the phone never stops and best of all we have eight definite suspensees and all paid up too.'

'All paid up? – how?'

'Insurance policies in our favour- cash- that sort of thing. Toast for you?' Basil nodded gloomily. Clarissa poured tea for them both and made toast. When it was ready she put it on the table along with a tray containing jam, marmalade and many small bottles of pills. Basil buttered a slice of toast. Thoughtfully he said, 'Insurance policies?'

'Yes- insurance policies- something wrong with that?'

'My dear Clarissa, just imagine the poor families left behind after the breadwinner dies. The families who counted on that policy for survival. It's cruel, that's what it is and terribly unfair. While the suspense disports himself in liquid nitrogen, freely spending the insurance money- what is to become of them?'

'Who cares,' said Clarissa, 'they're still alive- it's their problem.' She looked significantly at Basil, 'You know there is something they could do- just imagine it Basil- they could actually go out and find work.'

'Is that supposed to be a hint by any chance- and a heavy handed one at that?'

'It's the possibility that had occurred to me but not to you I gather. I am working for the first time in my life and enjoying it enormously – I'm a new woman. You just might find Basil, that if you got involved in the earning of money rather then merely in the spending of it, the experience might do the same for you- as well as paying the taxes.'

Basil searched the table and shook his head, 'Where may I ask is the honey?' 'Not here, and my seaweed tablets are missing too. I'll call

Mrs. Jenkins.' She raised her voice, 'Mrs. Jenkins, would you be an angel and bring the honey and seaweed tablets, they're in the pantry in the vitamin cupboard.'

'You need a whole cupboard now for your health foods Clarissa? Looking after yourself is one thing but all this...' he indicated the pill bottles on the table, '...it's truly ridiculous. Whatever for? You've become obsessed.'

'No Basil, obsessed is the wrong word. Let's say carful. It's ironic really- working towards immortality for others has made me more aware of my own mortality. You see Basil the healthier the body when the time comes to freeze it- well, healthy relatively speaking I mean, then the more likely and the easier will be the resuscitation.'

Mrs. Jenkins, her duster under the arm, came into the kitchen, bearing the honey and a bottle of pills on a tray. 'Thank you so much Mrs. Jenkins,' said Clarissa, 'I can't do without my daily dose of seaweed- it's packed full of iodine- did you know that Basil?' Basil did not look up and munched on his toast and honey in silence. Clarissa reached for the glass of water and began to swallow pill after pill from the various bottles on the table. Mrs. Jenkins watched her with admiration. 'I don't know how you get so many pills down you m'lady.'

Between mouthfuls Clarissa said,

'It keeps me thin- by the time I've taken all these I can't eat.' She looked slyly at Basil.

'There you are' said Basil 'how unhealthy can you get- not eating indeed. You know you will poison yourself with these massive doses of vitamins you're taking. Do you realise it's quite possible to overdoes on vitamins?'

Mrs. Jenkins shrieked and dropped her duster. 'Ooh- whatever will they think of next- I've heard of heroin overdose and cough medicines and glue sniffing but vitamins- that's a new one on me. I wonder if the village boys have thought of it yet?'

'They will Mrs. Jenkins, they will,' said Basil 'if they can afford heroin, then these crippling, expensive vitamin pills should present no problem. By the way Clarissa did you realise that our chemist bills have gone through the roof?'

Clarissa deliberately ignored him.

'Mrs. Jenkins I wonder if you would do Dr. Huxley's room today- we're expecting him later.' Mrs. Jenkins picked up her duster and departed.

'To change the subject Basil, I see you and Steve were out jogging together this morning- fun was it?'

'It's not a matter of fun Clarissa, Steve needs the exercise. It's extremely stultifying work looking after Mother- she must get out and get some fresh air occasionally.'

'And you see to it that she does. You're so noble Basil- that's what continually surprises me about you- so noble and a gentleman to boot. A gentleman who keeps his word.' Basil's brow darkened and he spoke through clenched teeth, 'Steve will leave as soon as we find someone else. I promised you that Clarissa and I intend to keep my word. It's merely a matter of time. We cannot leave Mother alone, you know that- perhaps you would like to look after her?'

Clarissa shook her head, 'Time, it's just a matter of time. Poor time always gets the blame doesn't it Basil? The eternal excuse- people haven't got time, can't find time, lose it or let it slip through their fingers. And time isn't even real, something one can grasp or touch- it's just figures on a clock. Sometimes time flies, sometimes it stands still- with you Basil it's definitely out of joint.'

'Time is relative Clarissa, isn't that what Mr. Einstein told us? I do wish you'd go back to collecting clocks- now there was a real hobby- interesting and productive as well as lucrative. Some of your clocks have become quite valuable you know.'

'Why Basil how nice of you to encourage me. Quite a switch for you though isn't it? I seem to remember you and Zil begging me to stop. You intimated that I'd taken leave of my senses.'

'If I was wrong I'm sorry- none of us is perfect. But I may be forgiven for thinking that if you persist with this body freezing nonsense then you have indeed taken leave of your senses.'

'What you really think Basil is that clock collecting is the lesser of two evils- mainly because it's much cheaper. Isn't that so?'

'Clarissa please, I don't want to fight with you- I want to help you, that's all.'

'I don't need help Basil, I am quite able to spend my money without you. In fact I'm finding it incredibly easy. I may be guessing here but I think that's the rub, that's what is really worrying you isn't it my poor darling. But let me reassure you- I have not changed my will- at the moment it's still in your favour.' The sun rose in Basil's eyes.

'There that's better isn't it?' Clarissa, Basil noted was laughing- at him. He ignored the slight and went on, 'Then there's still hope that you may abandon this insane project? I suspect that you're not one hundred percent convinced- am I right Clarissa?'

'Perhaps Basil. Of course you must accept that even though the will is in your favour you may find that later I've spent every last penny.'

Chapter Fifteen

''Clarissa I find this new streak of cruelty, of ruthlessness in you most unattractive. These last months have certainly changed you.'

'Perhaps I'm not as malleable as before Basil, perhaps I'm standing on my own two feet, alone, without your constant guidance- if I can call it that. Interference might be a better word.' Basil felt a surge of hopelessness, he felt as though arguing with the new Clarissa was quite pointless. He felt too a new fear, the fear of losing her. He began a different tack, more reasonably, more calmly. 'Clarissa I'm sure all this is due to Huxley's influence. I tell you again I don't trust the man. He has a dangerous, frontier mentality. No doubt his ancestors swept across the plains in covered wagons, fighting the Indians all the way to the Pacific- demented, out of their minds- every last one of them.'

'But we must admire the ones who made it- the pioneers. They're the ones who made America the great country it is today. Hux is indeed a pioneer, a pioneer in cryonics and now- so am I.'

Basil drained his cup and stood up. After propaganda like that, (Huxley had certainly been busy) there was nothing left for him to say.

'I'll go and change- enjoy the rest of your pills my dear.'

CHAPTER SIXTEEN

Clarissa took the small package she had bought in London and walked briskly towards the Hall. The day was sunless but not unpleasant. There was no wind and the air was cool and fresh-invigorating after the London pollution. When they saw her coming the children ran out to meet her.

'Clarissa, Clarissa, guess what?'

'Slowly Harry, first give me a kiss, you too Henry and you Eddie. Now- what's the news?'

'Mummy and Daddy were shouting again- loudly we heard them didn't we Henry?'

'Yes we did- Mummy was screaming out words at the top of her voice...' Clarissa intrigued asked, 'what words was she screaming Harry?'

'She was screaming 'No- No- No I won't' she sounded just like Eddie when she's having a tantrum.'

'I don't have tantrums...' Eddie was furious, '... but Harry does. Mummy sounds just like Harry in a temper. I do not shout and scream, I don't do I Clarissa?'

Eddie, wounded, allowed herself to be comforted and embraced by Clarissa.

'I think you're all telling tales on poor Mummy and that's not really very nice is it? But what did Daddy say when Mummy said No, No?' Know-all-Harry couldn't wait to tell.

'Daddy said 'please, please Teresa just one more, just one more.' I think they hide secret chocolates in their bedroom so we won't get them, don't you think that Clarissa?'

Harry's ingenuous little face was troubled, she needed reassurance. The thought of her parents secreting chocolates was a true betrayal.

'They might...' Clarissa thinking on her feet could do no better than '...they might just be talking about...about going for a walk.' The children thought this over for a moment before rejecting the idea. They shook their heads and Harry said scornfully, 'I bet it's not that, I bet it's really chocolates; they're just big, selfish pigs.'

'Selfish pigs- just like Nanny said about Georgie,' echoed Eddie. Clarissa thought it wise to change the subject. 'Well girls, what's the new baby doing now?'

Chapter Sixteen

'Oh Geraldine is so boring she doesn't do anything at all. Just lies there and smiles' Lucky Teresa thought Clarissa. 'By the way where is mummy- I want to talk to her.'

'She's weeding in the walled garden.'

'I think I'll go see her there. Why don't you all run along now- Nanny will be wondering where you are. I'll come up to the nursery in a minute and we'll have a game of snakes and ladders before I go home- I promise.'

'Snakes and Ladders, Snakes and Ladders- goody, goody, goody.' Shrieked the children, much as Teresa must have shrieked 'No, no,' while warding off Zil's advanced and ran, still shrieking joyfully, back towards the house.

Clarissa found Teresa on her knees weeding the herbaceous border ready for the spring flowering.

'Hello Teresa, not planting parsley by any chance?'

Teresa burst into tears. Clarissa dull of remorse said, 'oh darling- it was just a joke, I didn't mean to upset you. What's wrong- Zil being beastly?' Teresa wiped her eyes and blew her nose.

'I'm sure you can guess what it's all about Clarissa. Zil won't let up. He's determined that we must have another try for a boy. He won't leave me alone- he's practically raping me every other night. I can't keep fighting him off any longer- what shall I do Clarissa- I'm desperate.'

'Contraception?'

'He throws my pills away even though I've been hiding them and then I don't know where I am- except that I'm all out of kilter. He's wearing me down Clarissa- it's a nightmare.'

'You poor darling- I realise it's a dilemma for you. I suppose when it comes right down to it you have very few choices.'

'I have no choice Clarissa. The only alternative to what Zil wants is to leave him. And how can I possibly do that? It's out of the question- so I'll have to go through with yet another pregnancy and yet another disappointment.'

'Not necessarily- Teresa, I have a present for you. Maybe not a present you will like, but it's a chance you might like to take.'

Clarissa told her about the visit to the health food store, leaving out no smallest detail and soon Teresa was laughing again. They opened the parcel together and examined the contents. It consisted of several small packets of herbs, herbs unknown in texture and colour to either of them, while the overall smell was pungent and totally repulsive. Directions were included and advised steeping one set of herbs in hot water for three days before drinking three times a day, half an hour before meals until finished.

The other was to be pounded in a pestle and mortar and spread on pumpernickel. This last twice a week before breakfast. It was also advised to eat as much salt and horseradish as possible. If these directions were followed to the letter a boy (guaranteed) would result. The idea being that female sperms would be reduced in number and motility by this diet thus ensuring the fertilizing of the egg by a male sperm. Teresa said thoughtfully, 'You know Clarissa Daphne gave me a book detailing the conditions of intercourse which are supposed to do the same thing. One is supposed to work out when one ovulates- it's really complicated.' She gave a huge sign, 'But I suppose I will have to have another try. Though the conditions on both counts, the diet and the other seem to be utterly revolting...' the smell alone- however will I manage it?'

'I have an idea,' Clarissa was laughing in anticipation, 'why don't you put it to Zil that you are preparing to try for a boy again but that certain conditions pertain. Tell him that you have consulted the experts and you think it is possible to make a boy but you must have his complete support in the whole matter. Naturally he must share the diet- that is obvious. And he must follow your instructions on intercourse. What do you think of that?'

'Oh Clarissa you are wonderful- you've cheered me up immensely. I can't wait to see Zil's face when he realises he must drink the evil herb liquor. And not only that- he simply hates horseradish. I will give him some at every opportunity.' She hugged Clarissa, 'You are clever Clarissa- thank you.'

'Let's hope it works my dear. By the way the colourful witch in the health food store recommends intercourse to take place especially at full moon- I'll be thinking of you. And now I've promised the children a game of Snakes and Ladders. Come and play too.'

CHAPTER SEVENTEEN

Mrs. Jenkins stood at the stove in the kitchen of the Gates House stirring the lemon curd. It was her specialty. She stirred and watched as the canary coloured liquid began to thicken. In the oven the pastry case was browning. She was making a lemon meringue pie for the American. She was to show him that the English could turn out a pie every bit as good as 'Mom's apple pie.' That's what her ladyship had told her and though she was not quite sure of the meaning of the phrase she was determined to make her special pie especially good. The lemon curd was ready. Mrs. Jenkins took it off the stove and examined the pastry case. It too was ready and she removed it from the oven and put it on the bench to cool. Then she prepared the tray for afternoon tea. Three cups today as her Ladyship was expecting The American. Despite knowing his name perfectly well Mrs. Jenkins still thought of him exclusively as The American- the American with that very strange accent. As for his clothes- those shorts with buttonholes and buttons on the ends of the collar, and pink for heavens sake- and his looks so very foreign, and his manner of speaking- straight off the telly really.

In the sitting room Basil sat reading the Times. Clarissa was poring over an account book. The only sound was the ticking of the many clocks, a sound they had both become used to and no longer heard. Clarissa spoke.

'Basil…'

'Would you believe it Clarissa- some ancient vicar in Essex has already heard the first cuckoo- quite early this year- it's hardly spring yet.'

'Basil- I've told Steve to take Elizabeth's tea upstairs. She seems to have been behaving in a more bizarre manner than usual this week.'

'Steve? Is behaving more what…?'

'Not Steve Basil- Elizabeth. Yesterday when our worthy vicar came to tea- by the way do tell him about the cuckoo he will be furious that he didn't hear it first himself this year- when he came to tea; Elizabeth made some extremely lewd suggestions to him- most of which he fortunately failed to understand. When she received no feedback of the kind she was angling for, she removed her knickers and waved them around. At least they were black lace. I wasn't quick enough to stop her. The vicar almost fainted with embarrassment and was suddenly so breathless I feared for his heart. I do not want to subject Hux to the same treatment.'

'It would be good for him-might cause him to break into one of his rare smiles. He's a very earnest gentleman Clarissa- you must find him terribly tedious- don't you?'

'Not at all. He often laughs and makes jokes- you don't know him Basil. And you're challenging him. I think he finds you intimidating and that disconcerts him.'

'Aha- I disconcert him do I? What a pity.'

'Basil please don't be so horrid, he'll be here in a minute.'

'But Clarissa I thought Americans were quite unable to be intimidated by anyone, particularly not by us English.'

'He's a very sensible man Basil…'

'That is sentimental claptrap Clarissa- Americans are supposed to be tough and believe me they are. Tougher than you in your blind acceptance of this man, imagines. Just you wait and see…ah- here is our tea.'

Mrs. Jenkins entered with the tea tray and lad out the cups and milk and sugar on a small side table. At that moment the doorbell rang.

'That will be Dr. Huxley Mrs. Jenkins- show him in please and then you may bring the teapot.'

Mrs. Jenkins put the tray under her arm and went to the door. Charles Huxley came in and as he greeted Mrs. Jenkins he was reminded again that here, in the spectacle of Mrs. Jenkins was a major part of England personified. The hair in huge rollers under a purple scarf, the floral pinny, the tray under her arm at the ready. At the door of the sitting room he paused and looked at the two Hare Bells secure in their own domain. Basil in comfortable corduroys, Clarissa in tweed skirt, floral liberty blouse and around her neck the ubiquitous pearls. Many years of unchanging tradition were clearly visible in that picture. They both rose to greet him, Clarissa offered her cheek, Basil, reluctant, but still the gentleman, shook his hand. Then Charles, as though he had over heard the Hare Bell's conversation, and bravely for him, attempted a joke.

'Hi Clarissa- hi, Sir Basil- Clarissa tells me you are still jogging Sir Basil; still tempting fate then?' Basil did not smile.

'And you Dr. Huxley- still dealing in death?'

'Not death Sir Basil- life. Life everlasting.'

'I admire your eternal optimism Dr. Huxley, it seems nothing can demolish that. Ah- here is our tea.'

Mrs. Jenkins brought the hot teapot, extra hot water, thinly sliced bread and butter and a fruitcake.

'Thank you Mrs. Jenkins that looks lovely.'

'Will that be all m'lady?'

'I think so Mrs. Jenkins- all well in the kitchen?'

'I've put the macaroni cheese in the oven ready to heat and the pie is in the pantry- all done.'

'Sounds wonderful. Enjoy your evening,' To the others she explained, 'Mrs. Jenkins is playing Bingo in the village hall tonight. So we'll see you in the morning then Mrs. Jenkins. Good luck for tonight.'

'I'll need it m'lady. Goodbye all.' She departed and almost immediately they heard the sound of a car starting and with a scream of tortured tyres the noise, followed by its resounding echo, disappeared down the drive.

'The rollers in the hair are explained then,' said Basil. 'Unfortunately Dr. Huxley, the formality of our life has vanished- things are not as they used to be- and neither is the gravel on the drive. It will require raking again.'

He shook his head and sighed.

'I have spoken to Mrs. Jenkins about her driving Basil but she is always in such a hurry with so many things on her plate, as she puts it, that my admonitions seem to make no impact. But I need her so badly, that I must be very careful not to upset her or worse, antagonize her.'

'As you see Dr. Huxley that is our lot in life- never antagonize the servants no matter what monstrous deeds they perpetrate, nor what weird get-up they affect. Not like in the old days. Then they were required to wear a uniform- black frock, white lace collars, frilly white aprons and white caps on their heads- very fetching they looked too.'

He signed again. Charles attempted to envision a Mrs. Jenkins thus attired and failed- the picture was beyond his imagination. 'I need Mrs. Jenkins Basil- I have no intention of letting her go. She can wear a clown suit for all I care.'

'That my dear Clarissa is exactly what she looks like- a clown and I must put up with that abomination as well as being obliged to re-rake the gravel on the drive.'

Clarissa ignored Basil's complaints, poured tea and offered bread and cake. Charles accepted a small slice of cake which on tasting he found very dry and full of poisonously red glace cherries, the taste and texture of which he loathed. Fleetingly he thought of his mother's chocolate brownies- they seemed from another world entirely.

'I hear business is booming Dr. Huxley. Have you frozen anybody yet? I say Any Body advisedly.' Charles laughed. 'I'm glad to see you so cheerful Sir Basil. We are indeed very lucky. Eight definite suspensees and the phone doesn't stop. If it wasn't strictly confidential at this stage I could tell you their names. Some very famous people are more than interested.'

'So Clarissa assured me. And all paid up too I hear.'

'Not quite all. Some are still considering their options very carefully too; after all it's a big decision and, as we are all agreed, an expensive one.'

'You can say that again.'

'That's enough Basil, Hux is trying to explain...'

'I can tell you Sir Basil, that one of our definite suspensees is a very famous film actor. He is out of work at the moment and getting on a bit too. He is now at an age where the lack of work and poor publicity is hurting him. This lack could mean fabulous publicity for us if, to redress this state of affairs, he talks to the media at length about his plans. Knowing him I anticipate that he very soon will.'

''Or even better if he dies. Tell me Dr. Huxley who owns this famous about to be frozen body?' Basil's curiosity had got the better of his manners.

'I really can't tell you- you that Sir Basil- it would be breaking a confidence.'

'Clarissa- you tell me- you must know who it is?'

'Basil I'm sorry but I can't tell. I have been sworn to secrecy.'

'God in heaven you two are boring. But perhaps you can tell me something else Dr. Huxley- where will you store the bodies when you eventually tear them from the brinks of the grace?'

'Last week we purchased a disused warehouse in the East End of London. Now we are recruiting helpers. Over the next few weeks will fit the building out with the necessary machinery. We can store fifty cryocapsules or dewars as they are also called, in that very large space. They will of course be housed in special jar-free cradles and connected to all the relevant liquids and gases.'

'Jar-free cradles? Whatever for?'

'Well- in case the dewars are jarred in any way.'

'Jarred? How?'

'By any sudden movement- like- like...' Charles was stumped but only for a moment, '...by an earthquake for instance.'

'An earthquake? In the East End of London?' Basil's smile was more like a sneer. Charles ignored the implications. 'Who knows what may happen sir Basil- an earthquake, a bomb, or even a riot. We must be prepared for any and every eventuality. Our suspensees are entitled to expect that we will look after them as though they are made of the most delicate, the most precious of porcelains.' Basil continued to smile, but gently. Clarissa knew that smile, it boded ill for Hux.

'I do understand that you have many problems, Dr. Huxley' said Basil quietly, 'but I have thought of an idea that might interest you. Now, why not produce 'His' and 'Her' cryocaspsules- this measure could be an incentive- could be a terrific selling point. Just think of it- two bodies frozen at once.' Charles did not disguise his disgust but Basil, remorseless when ahead, continued, 'After all you must admit that the concept of 'His' and 'Hers' is originally an American idea, is that not so?' Charles ignored Basil and bowled a leg spin of his own.

'Clarissa- I bring good news from London. We take delivery of our mobile van next week.' Basil was forced back to his former argument.

'Ah indeed- the van. Tell me Dr. Huxley what wildly expensive equipment does it contain?' Happily Charles explained in unnecessary and gruesome detail.

'Well Sir Basil the van is especially fitted out to receive the body as soon as possible after death. Our unique refrigeration equipment will immediately chill the suspense, while the heart-lung machine will keep the blood circulating, as well as administering vital oxygen to the brain during the cooling process. This is a very important step, preventing brain damage due to oxygen starvation. Then the body is drained of blood with our special blood draining equipment, injected with a blood substitute and laid out on dry ice. All of that is done in the van.' Basil's brow darkened as he listened. Cheerfully Charles continued, 'The preparation of the body ready for interment in the capsule, the injecting of it with the special chemicals and placing it in a Dacron wool sleeping bag which stays soft at minus 196 degrees Centigrade, is done later at the warehouse. Of course I need hardly add that the van is radio controlled.' Basil's eyes had narrowed further during Charles' explanation. His last weapon was a weak attempt at irony.

'With especially expensive radio receiving equipment no doubt.' Clarissa and Charles remained unmoved.

'Hux that is wonderful news- to have the van ready to go at a moments notice will make our suspensees feel very much safer.' Basil broke in, 'Did you say safer- that's a contradiction in terms.'

'It's basic Basil- it makes us feel safer while their still alive and waiting to be suspended, to know that we can be frozen with a minimum of damage to our cells and tissues. It will make the thawing out process so much easier.'

'I continue to be amazed at your confidence, you two. What makes you so sure that someone will defrost you in this mythical, distant future?'

'Sir Basil I must assure you that revival will be no problem. Our society has a moral and legal obligation to attempt to recover its suspensees. The system is self-perpetuating. New generations will care for the suspensees, will themselves be suspended and in turn be cared for, until eventually the time will come for...' Basil interrupted rudely, '...for defrosting. Think of it both of you- thousands of vacuum flasks, in their jar-free cradles, full of diseased, disabled, geriatrics. Who will need them? I venture to say most certainly not our healthy young descendants.' Clarissa, unsure now said, 'more tea anyone...Basil all those people will be needed I'm quite positive... with their wisdom... and experience of...well...the old days...' She poured tea for herself with a hand that shook ever so slightly. 'Balderdash Clarissa. Do you really imagine that they will want Dr. Huxley's wisdom? In scientific terms he will be rated about as highly as a Neanderthal. Or an ageing film stars wisdom? Wisdom of what? And yours perhaps? And none of you even healthy. All of you old, sick and worn out. Your only possible value as I see it would be as side-show exhibits in a circus, and even that benefit must be rated as doubtful. There will be many far more fascinating and unusual things to titillate the public's interest by then, I'd bet on it. Martians perhaps.'

'Tea...' said Charles desperately '...I'd love some more Clarissa.' Clarissa poured tepid tea. Basil continued with increased confidence, 'Face it- you will be totally obsolete and so will all your suspensees. I predict that future generations will pull the plugs on you, on all of you.' Visibly shaken Charles and Clarissa sipped cold tea with a show of bravery.

'Take no notice of him Clarissa, I have faith in humanity and in Immortality Inc. Our members will stand by each other I'm sure of it.'

'With the world as overcrowded as it already is? I think not Dr. Huxley. I would make that bet on it, and a large one to boot, expect that I'm afraid, I wouldn't be able to collect. If I were you Clarissa I'd forget the whole damn thing.'

'Don't worry Hux, I'm not listening, I will stand firm. Someone must pioneer new ideas. That, of course is the hard part- pioneering. Ridicule, Basil, is easy.'

'Not so easy- not everyone can do it as effectively as I can.' Basil, spurred on by the effect his words were having on Charles and Clarissa went on, 'Now Dr. Huxley, if you really want to make a success of this cryonics rubbish I have another idea for you. Why wait for death? Why freeze dead bodies? Freeze live ones. Freeze healthy young bodies. A guaranteed healthy suspense would have a better chance of being revived wouldn't you say?' Charles replied heatedly, 'That's preposterous- who would willingly submit themselves to that?' 'Aha – Dr. Huxley you see the flaw in your own argument then. You agree that revival may not be automatic or even possible?' Charles, flummoxed remained silent, feverishly trying to find a plausible rebuttal. Basil drove on. 'Think of it- healthy, young, intelligent bodies. Think of the uses they could be put to.' Clarissa bewildered by the turn the argument had taken asked, 'But who…how…?'

'Why not you Clarissa- you're not so young but you're reasonably healthy. How?- well I'll tell you, you get your affairs in order, make your will, throw a farewell party and call the refrigerated van. Before you can say Jack Robinson your veins have been emptied of blood and there you are in your cosy sleeping bag floating happily in your jar-free vacuum flask.' Charles shook his head and opened his mouth but Basil, in full flight now sped on, 'or consider this- an unemployed, healthy, young drop-out on the verge of turning to drugs to solve his problems- a parasite feeding on society you will agree. His rich parents might decide he would stand a better chance of life in the future- a chance to make something of himself. They could sign him up- have a farewell party and so on. You would probably get hundreds of applications, particularly if you advertised on say, the following lines. 'Put your problems in suspended animation- allow the future to deal with them…'

Clarissa rose to her feet.

'That's enough Basil- you're being purposely outrageous. None of what you propose is worth considering. It's worse than euthanasia, in fact it's practically murder.' 'Euthanasia, murder- why not? That's a sound idea Clarissa. If you want to get rid of someone and you can afford it, bop them on the head, call the van and that's it. At last we have a new and foolproof way to dispose of the body.' Basil had gone too far and he knew it. Charles said quietly, 'that wouldn't work Sir Basil. We are required by law to have a death certificate before freezing. The same applies to your healthy young bodies idea.' Basil had been knocked out but would not lie down.

'Well- get the law changed, or find a way around it. It's too good an opportunity to miss. After all you need the customers. Your advertising could reach so many people so many different stratas of society- rich people, people jaded with life, people sick of it all. How about- become a suspense- wait in bacteria and viral free comfort for revival in a new, a better world. Die Now- Live Forever. More tea anyone?'

CHAPTER EIGHTEEN

In the yellow room Charles having dressed for dinner stood at the window watching the twilight. The days had become perceptibly longer but still darkened early and were still coloured a deep English grey. The trees too, quite bare, raised their long, skinny arms to the sky like supplicants begging heaven for spring. As the light over the gardens diminished, the overall greyness was accentuated and yet here and there small dots of yellow stood out- the first brave daffodils pushing their heads through the cold soil. But even those bright patches of colour did little to alleviate the bleakness of the scene- summer seemed a long way off.

There was a knock at his door and Clarissa came in and stood beside him at the window. In the gloomy distance the Hall dominated the landscape- standing foursquare and solid, everlastingly demanding of attention and time. Clarissa looked away from its lowering presence, looked up at Charles apologetically.

'Poor you Hux- Basil is becoming quite impossible. I apologise for him and for his disgraceful behaviour.' Charles put his arm around her shoulders and drew her to his side.

'Poor Clarissa, you mean,' She leant against him. His tall strength was a consolation; she felt comfortable, she felt as though she belonged there.

'Why do you stay with him Clarissa?'

'I can't run away now Hux, we've been together for too long. Poor Basil- I'm giving him a very hard time.'

'He's not exactly giving you a joy ride either Clarissa.'

'I know- but it's just that he hates his life to be disturbed and we are disturbing him immensely. We are threatening his very existence.'

'I feel threatened too Clarissa,' Charles needed reassurance, needed, he knew, Clarissa. He went on, 'I feel uneasy here, as though I am poaching on his preserve. Come back to London with me to stay. Please Clarissa.'

His arm tightened around her. She did not answer but did not pull away. In the twilight her face as she turned to him was quite beautiful. At her ears the Hare Bell pearls gleamed mysteriously.

The dining room of the Gate House while not as grand as the remarkable room at the Hall was at least warmer. At the table consuming Mrs. Jenkins's macaroni cheese was the whole Hare Bell family. Elizabeth at the far end reigned triumphant in a long black lace gown.

Chapter Eighteen

On her head she wore a huge black hat trimmed with red feathers which bobbed in time with her fork as it made its way to her mouth. Teresa and Zil who had been invited because their cook had been called away to minister her sick mother, were quite obviously not on speaking terms. It was clear too that Clarissa and Basil were similarly at odds. Charles mused on the blessed silence as he munched his way with some difficulty through the pale gluey mess on his plate. How he longed for a real American salad.

'My public...,' began Elizabeth 'needs me. I have decided to return to the stage. No...' she waved her fork at the company '...do not try to stop me. I have made up my mind. I will sing my song "If Those Hips Could Only Speak" written exclusively for me. Apocryphal of course since you all know, I can make my hips speak any time at all; when my hips utter I assure you they speak volumes!'

'More macaroni and cheese Mother?'

'No thank you Basil. Tell me my dear, who is that handsome man sitting there next to you Clarissa?'

'That is Dr. Charles Huxley- an American Mother.'

'How nice to meet a fellow American. How do you do Dr. Huxley.' Elizabeth extended her hand across the table, 'I suppose you have no difficulty in recognizing me. I'm the kind of girl who climbed the ladder of success, wrong by wrong.' She laughed, 'A simple joke Dr. Huxley but, au fond, quite true.' Clarissa attempted a diversion, 'More macaroni cheese Hux?' 'No thank you Clarissa, but it really was delicious.' Teresa added, 'Yes Clarissa it was quite delicious. Mrs. Jenkins makes a wonderful macaroni cheese. I only wish I could persuade Cook to make it like this, but our cook...' she explained to Charles, '...thinks she's the world's greatest operator in the kitchen and will not accept any new recipes. Hers date, not, unfortunately from Mrs. Beeton but from Cooks mother who hails from Scotland where the food is particularly hearty. Enough said. At least tonight, thanks to Clarissa's invitation, we have been spared the nursery food Nanny produces in a crisis- boiled eggs with toast soldiers followed by bread and milk.'

'I cannot for the life of me understand why you don't learn to cook Teresa.' Zil peevish was in a mood to complain. 'Because you keep me well and truly pregnant Zil, and when I'm pregnant I feel so sick that I cannot even set foot in the kitchen- much less cook.'

Steve began to clear the plates and Clarissa went to the kitchen to fetch the pie. The prevailing mood of the company when she set it on the table, lightened considerably. Even Basil smiled and said, 'Good- one of Mrs. Jenkins famous Lemon meringue pies.' Only Charles looked dubious. 'I ordered it especially for you Hux,' said Clarissa, 'knowing how fond Americans are of pie. I do hope it measures up.' Charles wondering how he was going to force down yet another Hare Bell concoction smiled weakly, 'I'm sure it will Clarissa.' Zil unwilling to concede his position in his private fight with Teresa continued nastily, 'Since you are not pregnant now Teresa, you might consider taking up the arduous task of learning how to cook.'

Clarissa signed as she cut the pie into wedges. The battle between those two was only just beginning. 'I might very well do just that Zil, since pregnancy, as a career, is definitely out of the question for me.'

'Come now Teresa,' said Basil, 'don't make hasty decisions. Pregnancy suits you, you always look absolutely blooming.'

'I'm sick and tired of looking like an overblown rose Basil. I've been nothing else for years. I want to be pale and thin and light as a feather.' Basil became more serious. 'Teresa, you must think of the Name, the Title. It's terribly important you know that. You must not give up so easily.' Outraged now Teresa said, 'Give up so easily Basil- I don't think anyone in their right mind could accuse me of giving up- have you peeped into the nursery lately…?'

'My dear Teresa no one could possibly accuse you of such nonsense,' Clarissa responded immediately and with a fire, 'Giving up indeed I'd like to see those two,' she pointed at Basil and Zil, 'giving birth year after year- they'd give up after one such experience I'm quite sure of that. Teresa I appreciate what you have done for this family even if Basil doesn't, and I agree with you- you have done more than enough. To hell with the Name, to hell with the Title. Anyways I don't see why girls can't carry Title.'

'Because it's the law.' Basil said dismissively, hoping to close this dangerous line of argument.

'Then the law should be changed.' Clarissa was not to be put off. Basil continued, 'Rubbish. It wouldn't be the same somehow, girls carrying the title and the name. No- it wouldn't work at all- it wouldn't be right.' Clarissa replied wearily, 'See what you're up against Teresa? A thousand year inheritance of unleavened, blind prejudice, Basil, I repeat, my question- why not let the girls carry the title?'

'Because its traditional for the name to be passed on through the male line. My dear ladies…' Basil looked condescendingly around the table, '…my dear ladies it would take an act of parliament, possibly dozens of acts of parliament to alter that tradition.' Now Charles, emboldened by the taste of the pie which was surprisingly good, said, 'I understand that over here, in this country of England, one cannot fight tradition. You girls might as well take on a saber-toothed tiger.' Basil replied smugly, 'You're absolutely right old boy, this is the beauty of tradition- it has strengthened, it is virtually indestructible, it lasts. In this temporary, throwaway society, tradition is the one worthwhile and valuable thing, the only one thing that lasts.' 'You see Hux,' Said Clarissa 'how tradition has become the opiate of the upper classes. With their minds firmly shut against progress they continue to perpetuate it. Sometimes I think it's their only reason for existence. Take away that prop and who knows…?'

'You may try Clarissa but you cannot destroy tradition in one stroke- it is too strong for you or for anyone else.'

'Not quite Basil, not always. It was traditional for women not to vote and look what happened to that custom. There's one prop knocked out and didn't it give all you traditionalist a fright.'

'Voting…' said Elizabeth darkly '…is devilish work.' Charles laughed, 'You are so right…er…Miss West.' 'What a nice, generous man you are- you understand me. Around here…' Elizabeth waved her spoon '…not many do understand me.' But Clarissa was not one to be steered away from her subject.

'The trouble with you two,' eyeing Basil and Zil, 'is that you so seldom appraise what it is you are trying to preserve. The law of inheritance of Title should be changed. Teresa, let's do something about it- someone should begin. Are you with me?'

'Clarissa will you please stop inciting Teresa. Leave her alone. She has quite enough to do looking after Zil and the girls without your stirring. You are a bad influence.'

Teresa, without hesitation responded immediately, 'I'm with Clarissa on this Basil, one hundred percent.' 'I'm surprised at you Teresa,' Zil was not surprised at all, merely extremely cranky, 'Surprised that you listen to my Mother's words, words which are uncharacteristic of her to say the least. I don't know where they come from.' He looked hard at Charles. Basil continued, 'I am sure that at heart Teresa you believe in tradition and all that it stands for, certainly you believe in the tradition of this family.'

'What rot,' Clarissa was fast losing her temper, 'tradition is like adultery- an indulgence few can afford and right now Basil, you cannot afford either.'

'We are seeing the new Clarissa with a vengeance. You don't let an opportunity slip by do you Clarissa? Never marry a woman with money Dr. Huxley, she will eventually use it as a whip to beat you with.'

'That's not true Basil- I've never attacked you on that score before, you must admit that.'

'True, but sooner or later you all do it- with most wives it's sooner- with you Clarissa I do admit it's been a late flowering vice.'

'Now we will have coffee in the siting room,' said Clarissa firmly and led them all away from the unleashed volatility of the table.

In the kitchen Teresa helped stack the plates in the dishwasher while Clarissa made coffee. As they worked they complained to each other about their husbands. This mutual disburdenment cheered them up but both knew that mere words would do little to change the narrowness, the imperviousness of the Hare Bell minds.

Coffee was taken with polite conversation, discussion centering on weather forecasts for spring, for the following week and for the next year. The easy English pretence that nothing of note, nothing of disharmony had happened a mere ten minutes ago took over. Then everyone wished everyone else a civil goodnight and went speedily to bed.

Clarissa and Basil undressed in silence, cleaned teeth in relative silence and climbed into bed. Clarissa picked up her book and began to read. Basil thrashed around restlessly for a minute and then reached for his wife. 'Let's not fight Clarissa, let's make peace.' She pushed him away with some force.

'What's wrong Basil? Steve not available tonight?'

'How can you say that- I've given her up I told you so. You do believe me?'

'No Basil, I do not believe you. You promised to sack Steve, and to find someone else to look after Elizabeth. I see no evidence that you have even begun to keep your promise.'

Basil squirmed silently. Clarissa continued, 'By the way there's another tradition that persists in this country with no sign of diminution- adultery. You Basil, perpetuate that tradition beautifully.' Basil unable to think of a telling retort, was forced back to the best defence, attack.

'Clarissa- I must say it again- you spend too much time in London with that American. It's not right. You are beginning to absorb his ideas. I don't like it.'

'I'm not bothered by what you like or don't like Basil. I have a new outlook on life, I am working on an enterprise in which I believe and that makes me happy.'

'But don't you realise Clarissa that Huxley is as queer as a five-toed frog.' Clarissa laughed aloud.

'Don't you mean toad?'

'Toad- whatever. But queer. He's a pansy. Why isn't he married, tell me that if you can. And he comes from San Francisco- everyone knows what goes on there.'

'I can assure you Basil, that Hux is not queer.'

Chapter Eighteen

'So he's made a pass at you?' 'No he has not,' Clarissa lied, 'He is an honourable man and as far as he knows I am securely married. But a woman can sense these things, he is certainly not queer.'

Basil congratulated himself. Cleverly he had achieved at least one of his objectives. He had established that Clarissa was faithful and likely, he optimistically assumed, to remain so. 'Oh well- as long as you believe it. I think I might just run up to London and have a look at this Immortality Inc. business for myself.'

He turned away from Clarissa, closed his eyes and was soon asleep. Clarissa remained awake for some time, mulling over the evenings conversation. Tonight, the same old clichés religiously mouthed by Basil and Zil were, on reflection sounding more hollow and more irrelevant than ever before. Perhaps Basil was right, perhaps she was beginning to absorb some of Hux's more sacrilegious ideas. She smiled at her thought and closed her eyes. Then she remembered Basil's threatened visit to London. She would try to dissuade him from taking this unprecedented step. Basil hated London it shouldn't be difficult she comforted herself and soon slept.

Up at the Hall Zil and Teresa undressed in silence, cleaned teeth in relative silence and climbed into the bed in which it was rumoured Bonnie Prince Charlie had once slept- and not alone. A pleasing little story which lent the Hall an added charm. Teresa picked up the book Daphne had given her and began to read. Zil thrashed about restlessly for a time and then reached for his wife. 'Leave me alone Zil. I've told you there will be no more of that nonsense unless...' Zil's face brightened. '...Unless what?'

'Unless you do exactly as you're told. First of all you must read this book.' Reluctantly Zil reached, instead of for his wife, for the book and began to read. He leafed through diagrams and graphs and unpleasant physical details rapidly, and groaned with an emotion Teresa interpreted as revulsion every time he turned a page. After five minutes he snapped the book shut and gave it back to her. He remained speechless, staring straight ahead with a face like a man who had ben stunned by a severe blow to the head. Teresa patted his cheek sympathetically 'My poor darling. But Zil do listen carefully. I have been researching the whole business of conception and providing you follow my directions I am prepared to try again- one last time.' Zil recovered well, reaching for her again. Teresa slapped his wandering hand sharply. 'Not now Zil, there's much that has to be established before any of that old hanky panky.' Zil's face resumed it's petulant mien.

'What? But I must say Teresa I am surprised that Daphne got hold of a book like that- it's almost pornographic.' 'Do you promise to listen intelligently and do as I tell you? Exactly and to the letter?'

'Yes Teresa I promise- now tell me- surely it can't be so difficult, or so repellent as it appears in that book.'

'You may be surprised Zil. Now first of all no more hot baths for you. It's cold baths exclusively from now on.' Zil opened his mouth to protest but the expression on Teresa's face caused him to shut it again Teresa continued, 'Hyperthermia, that means heat. For your information Zil heat is injurious to reproductive functioning in the male. Heat kills all sperm but kills the smaller, male producing sperm first. So excessive heat lowers the sperm the count thereby causing more girls to be conceived.'

'Really?' Zil looked suddenly anxious.

'Yes, really. More boys are produced when the male sperm reaches the egg first and that is helped by having them swim in an alkaline secretion. Therefore we need to increase the flow of alkaline secretions and we can achieve this by a special diet, preceded by various herbal infusions.'

'That sounds quite feasible, though I don't know about cold baths. I bet that's not necessary Teresa, if we do the other bit.'

'Alright then Zil if you can't make even one sacrifice we'll simply forget the whole thing…'

'No,…no Teresa- I promise to do whatever it takes.'

'You will have to accept Zil, that altogether this process is a very tiresome business. I will have to take my temperature every morning, as well as some other yukky details which I will spare you, in order to try to establish the exact time of ovulation after which…'

'…after which we have unlimited hanky panky?' Zil's hopes so minimally raised were about to be dashed, 'Not so fast Zil. You will be heavily restricted in that area- you must abstain from hanky panky in order to make as many sperms as you can. Then having established the exact time of ovulation we will have intercourse but once only, and then not all until the next ovulation, Otherwise we may get another girl.' Zil groaned.

'How incredibly romantic, I can't wait.'

'Don't sign Zil- there's one good bit- you may drink a couple of cups of strong coffee fifteen minutes before intercourse. Caffeine can have a stimulating effect on the male sperm- makes them swim faster.' Zil sighed, turned over and shut his eyes.

'Whatever you say Teresa- one hanky panky is better than none, that is if I will be able to perform at all after all that nonsense. You work it out. I am in your hands. Sleep well.' He won't call it nonsense thought Teresa as she turned over too, when he is faced with a herbal infusions, not to mention the horseradish.

In the yellow room Charles Huxley climbed into his lonely bed. He put his head onto the pillow and wondered why he had allowed himself to become so profoundly involved with the Hare Bells. The impact of Clarissa's name connected with his company Immortality Inc. was certainly a factor. But that aside, there was really no need for him to subject himself to these country weekends which were taking a severe toll on his nerves. Why was he torturing himself? Why did he submit to Basil's rudeness without instant retaliation- immediate action- like a swift punch on the nose which he would dearly love to have given him tonight. The answer was Clarissa. Deep in his heart he knew it was only Clarissa. Clarissa was so different from all other women he had known and it was not only the piquancy of her Englishness that made her so attractive. He was feeling more and more fiercely protective of her. Particularly when Basil attacked her so cruelly. He longed to remove her from the Hare Bell orbit, to take her with him back to London, or to San Francisco, or to anywhere at all. He longed to give her back her confidence, to watch her laugh more often, to watch as she absorbed new experiences, to give her a bright, a new life instead of the grey life she had always had. He signed and closed his eyes but the thunderous country night noises continued without pause and resounded and echoed in his head as he tried in vain to sleep.

CHAPTER NINETEEN

At breakfast on the following morning Charles Huxley marvelled anew. The sight of Mrs. Jenkins in a well-worn navy blue track suit, feather duster in hand like a flag, flitting about amongst the clocks , Clarissa in a surprisingly revealing black negligee, Basil and Steve, red and breathless in their sweaty running gear and Elizabeth in the same clothes she had worn the night before looking as though she had slept in them (she had) reminded him once more that he really was in England, the land foremost in the whole world in eccentricity. The thought was unsettling but he drank his orange juice with barely a shudder. 'Hux you look a little tired this morning.' Said Clarissa solicitously, 'after breakfast we will walk in the garden, you need fresh air. Then we will get down to doing our account books.'

'Whatever you say Clarissa- sounds nice.' Anywhere as long as it was away from Basil thought Charles. He ate scrambled eggs, scrambled some hours ago it seemed as they had the texture of rubber, served on soggy toast. As he swallowed he wished he was eating one of his mother's blueberry muffins. San Francisco, the apartment in Pacific Heights with the view over the bay, his mother's muffin's and his mother's coffee seemed as far away as the moon.

'Are you taking Elizabeth to the Jumble sale this afternoon Steve?' Asked Clarissa. Steve with a mouthful of egg nodded. Elizabeth pursed his lips with relish before she said, 'Goody, goody, a jumble sale. That will be fun. Am I selling kisses again?'

'Not today Mother,' said Basil wearily, and noting Elizabeth's crestfallen face went on, 'but I'm sure you will enjoy yourself just the same.'

'I will not- I just want to sell kisses it's what I always do at these public entertainments. It's expected of me.' 'The Vicar wouldn't like it dear,' said Clarissa. 'The vicar's not going to get it' replied Elizabeth and laughed uproariously. Clarissa felt it was time to go. 'Are you finished Hux? I think we might take our walk now.' Thankfully Charles left the remainders of his coffee and followed Clarissa into the garden. The day was again cold and grey though every now and then the sun peeped through the high cloud. At least, thought Charles, today there was none of England's endless, drizzling rain.

'Look Hux- a daffodil. Spring is here.' Charles decided then and there that there had been enough pretence, enough time wasted took Clarissa's hand in his.

Chapter Nineteen

'Clarissa, my dearest, that awful altercation last night, how can you bear it?'

'I suppose I'm used to it.' 'You must not put up with him any longer- it's not fair to you. Clarissa, I want you to leave Basil- I want you with me- for always.' 'Oh Hux- you are sweet but please don't rush me. I must be quite sure that what I do is right. You can understand that can't you? Twenty years is a very long time to share a life and not so easily dismissed. I must have sufficient reason...'

'Am I not reason enough?'

'Oh Hux you are, you are. But not yet. Please wait- I must be sure.'

'Clarissa, think of the time we are wasting- I want you with me, you need pampering. I want to show you the world- I want to give you all the things you've missed.'

'Please Hux, please don't press me- all this is so new to me- all these sensations I have are so novel. Let me savour them, let's take it slowly and enjoy ourselves without having to make any major, irrevocable decisions. Please Hux, give me time.'

'Time again, always time nipping at my heels like an impatient dog- it's been months Clarissa.'

'When one is happy time flies and cannot be counted or measured and that Hux is a fact' said Clarissa smiling, 'But Hux I must admit, I am happy, very happy. An entirely new feeling for me. I am finding it rather overwhelming.' Charles put his arm around her, 'At least Clarissa tell me that you will spend more time with me in London, time away from Basil. I hate to think of you here, with him, traditionally together as though set in stone lie that leaky old fountain.' Clarissa laughed, 'You paint a dreadful picture- does it really seem like that to you?' 'It surely does. Think of that picture Clarissa and then tell me that you will be with me more than you are with him. You know you do have plenty of justification to leave Basil altogether.' 'I promise to spend more time in London Hux. And I promise I will give you my answer when the time is right.' Charles cupped her face in his hands, 'The time is rarely right Clarissa- remember that it is only the here and now that matters.'

'And now here are the girls.' The three small figures came running down the path, Harriet well ahead of the other two. 'Look Clarissa- I found another one.' She waved a small glass ampoule which Clarissa took from her.

'No needle with this one?'

'No Clarissa.'

'Alright my darling. You'll get 20p for your moneybox. Does Nanny know?'

'Of course not- I'm too clever for her- I hid it under my pillow,' said Harriet smugly, very pleased to have outsmarted Nanny.

'Good girl Harry- and you too Eddie and Henry. Now tell me- how is Mummy this morning?' To Charles she whispered 'After their falling out last night…'

'She's in the kitchen.' 'That makes a change- is she actually cooking something?' 'I think so' piped Eddie, 'Whatever it is I hope we don't have to eat it' said Harry, 'It really stinks.'

'Yes- it really and truly stinks,' giggled Eddie and Henry, 'It stinks horribly, awfully, like…' 'That's enough Harry- we don't wish to know the details.' Clarissa interrupted just in time. Harriet ran on, 'Clarissa will you come and watch me riding in the gymkhana next Sunday?' Clarissa hesitated, and looked helplessly at Charles, 'Please Clarissa, please say yes…?'

'I'll try to be here darling. Run along now- Nanny will be wondering where you are.' They ran off with Daisy the old spaniel who had only just caught up with them, turning and lumbering along behind the three small figures.

'What on earth is that?' asked Charles eyeing the ampoule. 'It was Elizabeth's. When she was younger she had a flirtation with morphine. She used to hide these things all over the house and now the children keep finding them in the strangest places. Teresa and I don't want the staff to know so we and the girls have a little arrangement going…'

'But a flirtation? Is that what you call an addiction?' Charles was genuinely horrified.

'Well- perhaps a little more than a flirtation. Later she was successfully detoxed at the London Clinic without ill effects. There were many similar cases in those days you know Hux- morphine was quite easy to get- much like any modern drug today. Many of those well bred young ladies were incredibly wild in the twenties.'

'I guess we had some of the same at home- though I must admit my mother and her sisters were very proper young ladies.' Charles sighing loudly went on, 'And probably very boring- in fact much like me.' 'Stop fishing Hux- you are anything but boring and you know it. But you see how it is for me- now the girls want me at the gymkhana next week, and something else I haven't told you. Basil has threatened to come up to London for a visit. He says he wants to see how what makes Immortality Inc. tick. Actually I believe he's coming to check up on us. Oh Hux, what am I to do?' Her helplessness was touching. Charles took charge. 'Clarissa you must stay for the Gymkhana- Harry would be so disappointed if you were not there to watch her. And I certainly do not want to be the cause of her eternal enmity. I can wait, I have infinite patience- up to a point.' 'Hux you are a dear and in the meantime I will try to dissuade Basil from his snooping trek. He hates London, always has done so it may not be too difficult.'

'I will expect you next week then and Clarissa...'

'Yes Hux?'

'Remember that I am waiting for you, remember that it's here and now that really matters.'

CHAPTER TWENTY

Clarissa opened the gate to the gardens of the Cadogan Square with the key Charles Huxley had given her and skirting various doggy doos walked across the grass to the bench under a tree. The day was fair and windless, almost warm, almost like a real summer day. So it should be in August she thought. Some months ago Charles had given up his room at the Savoy and was renting a spacious flat which looked onto the leafy square. Clarissa when she came to London on Immortality Inc. business stayed with him. Separate bedrooms she assured Basil who did not believe her but was forced to remain silent, indeed acquiescent since Steve still ruled his own bed; an arrangement which now suited Clarissa very well. It allowed her the freedom to come and go from the Gate House as she pleased and liberated her from Basil's all consuming presence there. In there circumstances (which, at the moment, he was unwilling to abandon) Basil's objections to Immortality Inc. had declined to a rather hallow but irritatingly repetitive carping.

Today, Clarissa sitting in the gardens with the sun on her face tried not to think of tomorrow when Basil was at last due to make his threatened visit to London. Six months had gone by and Clarissa, though she had discouraged him successfully during that time, had been unable finally to persuade him that his trip was totally unnecessary. As well, the realisation that time was passing too quickly and that Charles Huxley would not wait for her forever was becoming burdensome. Already with the success of the London branch of Immortality Inc. there was talk from the head office of the opening of further branches in Asia and Australia which would require Charles to travel and to leave London, perhaps permanently. It was a dilemma that required a resolution- a decision, a decision she had allowed herself to postpone over and over again.

She thought back to how it had been over all the years with Basil. Her unquestioning acceptance of her life with him at the Hall, the birth of her son, her good works in the village, the years going by with a rapidity which now, on looking back, astounded her. Her life had been overwhelmingly dull, so much was true, but it had been safe, it had been secure. Secure, at a price. Even the greater pleasures of London had been denied her. Basil's thoughtful opinion of the theatre- poofters writing about poofters, acted by poofters, watched only by poofters- precluded such visits. The same was true of the opera and of course the ballet was quite out of the question. Country life was, according to Basil, the only life. Shooting birds, hunting foxes, farming and all this in the best and freshest air was real life as he and many of his neighbours saw it and lived it. Clarissa, who had embraced this existence without question, without self-assertion for so long had, over the past months been made hugely aware of an altogether new life, a possible new life with Charles Huxley. The thought of it loomed enticingly, promising adventures she had yearned for and never dreamt of achieving and yet she was afraid, afraid, like a child, of the dark, afraid of the unknown. To be suspended in a cryocapsule waiting indefinitely for a new and better life had once seemed alluring, had seemed an answer to her longings, to her discontent. But that was before Hux. Now the idea of life in an uncertain tomorrow was beginning to pall. A living breathing life was what she craved and at the same time feared. She shrugged the thought off again. First she must deal with Basil's visit, later when there was proof, proof of some kind that her leaving of Basil was right for her and for the family, that it was not the betrayal she knew it would seem, then she would make her decision. A betrayal- the word, even in thought hurt her, though honest as she was with herself she knew it to be particularly true. Basil had relied on her for so long, relied especially on her money that she was loath to deprive him of its comfort. Despite his many affairs which Hux continually held up to her, despite his cavalier treatment of her, until somehow she could see herself as justified, until she could stop pitying him in his obsessions, only then could she leave him.

Teresa Hare Bell and Daphne Tilletson sat together in a cosy corner of Ye Olde Buttercup Tea Roome on one of the rare days when they were able to be together without their many children; when they were able to talk together without constant interruptions, when they were able to enjoy a modicum of peace.

The Buttercup Tea Roome in the village was pure twentieth century olde English with sham low wooden beams across the ceiling and bottle glass in the windows. As well as a picturesque fireplace (which worked) there was one counter displaying village arts and crafts- pottery, macramé, jams and preserves all fashioned by local inhabitants for sale to customers.

The Buttercup was much frequented by accidental tourists who chanced upon the village and this, its only refreshment venue, on their way to more serious sight-seeing. Today a Nipponese bus tour had arrived and the many Japanese tourists were vying with one another to purchase genuine English craft and photographing this authentic piece of Olde England. Apart from each other there was much to immortalize on film. The tables were set with yellow table linen and the waitresses in yellow tights, hip length yellow skirts and anachronistic mob caps, flitted swiftly from table to table like frenetic canaries. One such, the proprietress of the business was certainly booming today.

'What'll it be ladies?' 'Are the scones fresh Patsy?' 'Out of the oven not five minutes ago.' 'Daphne, should we...?' 'Oh lets. Devonshire tea for two please Patsy.' Patsy frowned and said, 'I've got a lovely fresh spinach salad, served with calories free and fat free rice crackers. Much better for you and your unborn babies.'

'Patsy you are a busy body as well as a spoilt sport. You know we are usually terribly good and eat your politically correct salad without complaint. Occasionally we need to cheat on our diets a little, if only to retain our sanity.' Patsy relented and disappeared to fetch their order. Teresa turned to Daphne, 'Do you think she'll tell Tony- he comes in here occasionally between house calls.'

'I don't care if she does tell on us,' replied Daphne 'I'm fed up with being virtuous; In fact I'm fed up with being pregnant. This is definitely the last time for me.' Patsy soon returned with a tray loaded with warm scones thick clotted cream and the Tea Roome's own homemade strawberry jam. Teresa and Daphne each took a warm scone, piled on the jam and cream and giggled like schoolgirls as they crammed the scrumptious morsels in their mouths. 'We shouldn't be doing this,' said Daphne through an ambrosial mouthful. 'I suppose that's why it tastes so divine.' 'Tony would kill us if he could see us now... I can hear him saying- Daphne, you've put on too much weight this month- what have you been doing? And then what I say "merely keeping my body and soul together Tony- you know- eating?" He frowns and says "don't joke Daphne- you must keep your weight down for your own health and for the health of your unborn child.'

'I know- the man has no sense of humour as well as being a slave driver.'

'We only do this once in a while- it can't hurt. Anyway it's blissful to cheat.'

'You know Daphne, these days everyone seems to be on some diet or other; and with everyone consuming hundreds of vitamin pills the diet industry must be making a small fortune.'

'Many small fortunes- as many as there are different diets, and new and fashionable eating fads. The latest craze is no fat and lots of fibre. Dominic and Serena are totally obsessed with fat and fibre.'

'Isn't that beans and more beans?' Asked Teresa, 'Yes and we all know the unwelcome product beans occasions.' Teresa laughed. Daphne continued, 'They were at the Mainwarings dinner party a couple of weeks ago. It was a scream. Serena produced a little book and told us exactly how much or how little fibre or fat was in every mouthful we consumed. And they both refused the chocolate mousse with whipped cream- Lucy was furious.' 'Now I know the origins of the rumour that Dominic and Serena are persona non grata at local dinner parties.' 'Are you surprised? But tell me Teresa does Zil know about the baby yet? If Patsy knows of your pregnancy surely so must the whole world.' 'So far I haven't told him and he's so unobservant he hasn't even guessed. I'm still making him drink the herbal infusions, take only cold baths and eat horse radish- all that stuff. At last I have been able to make him participate in my pregnancy in a tangible way and I'm loving it. You know Daphne, he is remarkably faithful to my every demand despite his continuing nausea. He is so keen I find it truly amazing. And best of all there has been another unforeseen benefit- I think it's highly probable that he would refuse to submit himself to this whole disagreeable process all over again; so this will be our last baby.' 'Lucky you. I know that Hugo will not stop till we have our daughter. You know Teresa I finally had to tell him that I was pregnant- in fact he guessed. I was not good at disguising my rapidly enlarging tummy.'

'But then you are further on than me- when is the long awaited daughter due?'

'In the middle of October. But fingers necessarily crossed for the daughter.'

'But Daphne you did it all by the book didn't you?'

'For a while- then we sort of petred out. Now I'm just hoping. What about you- tell me honestly- did you really stick to that grueling regime?'

Teresa helped herself to more jam and more cream and slathered the lot onto half a warm scone. She took a bite before replying.

'To tell the absolute truth Daphne- and I am swearing you to secrecy on this- we mostly did, but there was one time after we'd had a particularly good bottle of wine at dinner, actually two bottles now that I come to think of it, that I gave in to an unprecedented wave of passion and very unfortunately when I checked the book it was not the right time. I am fairly sure it was on that particular night that I conceived. But I'm still hoping too- at least there was a full moon that night!' Daphne laughed, 'So you're in the same boat- the one in which we sail with fingers crossed.'

'Yes- but even on pain of death I would never admit it. I will not tell Clarissa either- if we get a boy, I would want her to take most of the credit.'

'You know Teresa I think you should take pity on poor Zil- tell him you are pregnant and stop making him drink all those awful mixtures.'

'Perhaps you're right Daphne. Anyways I'm tired of wearing big shirts. Mind you no one at the Hall ever seems to look at me. Basil and Zil are totally immersed in their own affairs and then there are the girls who take their minds off me. I may tell him tonight after his last cold bath, though I'll give it further thought- I'm enjoying his discomfort too much at the moment.'

'You're a sadist Teresa- he's suffered long enough. But more importantly, we need more jam and more cream.' Said Daphne recklessly and beckoned one of the canaries.

CHAPTER TWENTY-ONE

IMMORTALITY INC.
President Dr. Charles Huxley.
Vice President Lady Clarissa Hare Bell.

Basil read this sign inlaid in brass on the warehouse doors and pressed a button which rang a bell somewhere in the building. When Charles Huxley opened the door Basil ignored the outstretched hand, indicating instead the sign and exclaimed in his most pompous way, 'Well Dr. Huxley from this brass plate I infer that the combination of American know-how and English aristocratic tradition is at work.' He rubbed his hands together in a self-congratulatory way and went on, 'you are certainly making the most of your connections- but I suppose, or should I say, I guess, it's the American way.' Charles, used by now to Basil's insolence said simply, 'come in Sir Basil, come on in. We have been expecting you.' He ushered him through the door deliberately ignoring the insults. Basil's manner was no longer able to surprise. He continued with equanimity, 'Clarissa is here briefing the leader of our new support group; we have instituted counseling for the relatives and friends of our suspensees.' Basil's face reflected his disbelief.

'Counseling- surely a further unnecessary expense?' 'Comfort and consolation is our motto Sir Basil and all our people, be they alive or suspended will have the complete and entire benefit of our experience in these matters.' Basil shook his head- Americans, particularly salesmen were masters of tautology. He followed Charles into a significantly carpeted (the best Axminster in a neutral and coloured shade) ante chamber. Fresh flowers, white lilies, stephanotis and white roses filled the air with a mixture of sweet and cloying scents. The atmosphere was like that of an elaborate funeral parlour, American style, thought Basil. The roses were doubtless without thorns, another American invention. They went on through to an even larger room furnished with comfortable easy chairs and low tables. In one corner stood a huge black marble topped desk, rather reminiscent of a giant tombstone. Upon its polished surface stood a computer, an elaborate silver desk set and two white telephones. 'My office,' explained Charles unnecessarily.

'We have given up the original rooms we were renting in Chelsea since here, as you see, we have so much more space.' There was an open door leading into yet another room from which issued a very loud and strident voice in determinedly cheerful vein, '…be assured Lady Clarissa I understand the problem we face. Empathy is the name of the game. I have been trained to intuit all possible emotions and to project that knowledge. Purposeful expression of feelings, acceptance of the impending death, non-judgmental attitudes, will all be on offer. Of course no negative thoughts will be harboured- negativity of any persuasion will not be allowed…' '…Perhaps, a less authoritarian slant would be a kinder way to go,' interrupted Clarissa, '…and please do remember Cynthia that the deceased, our client is not actually dead- he or she is a suspensee. The relatives will later be suspended too and will expect to be reunited with our clients in the future when all of them will be revived together. We stress the reuniting scenario. What they need at this poignant moment is, in the main, encouragement.' Encouragement to part with their money thought Basil uncharitably.

'That will do for now Cynthia- we will have further discussions later.' Cynthia duly put in her place remained silent. As Lady Hare Bell, Clarissa had a masterful presence. She emerged from the room and smiled at her husband.

'Hello Basil- I gather you made it to the sinful, polluted city of London without incident?'

'My dear Clarissa…' for once, Basil faced with a suddenly competent, in charge wife, was bereft of words. He approached her gingerly and kissed her check, wondering not for the first time where the money for all this opulence sprang from, hoping it was not all from Clarissa's dowry. It was as though Charles had read his mind.

'We are an American company Sir Basil- the money for this establishment is issued to our branch by Immortality Inc. U.S.A.- we are already a very rich company as you will see when I show you the rest of our enterprise.'

Like Clarissa, thought Basil, Charles was more in charge here than he had ever seen him. In charge of this domain of death- or was it of life, as both Clarissa and Charles maintained. Basil did not speak. His silence was uncharacteristic, his face reflected his confusion. All at once he was a deflated balloon and Clarissa felt the familiar stirring pity for him. Charles was aware of her mode. He saw the danger and determined to bring him back to his aggravating and sarcastic self as quickly as possible. 'Now Sir Basil, we will show you the suspensees room. Unfortunately the fully fitted ambulance, with fully operational heart lung machine, radio controlled of course, courtesy of Clarissa as you know, is on call at the moment but I may be able to show it to you later.'

Chapter Twenty-One

The thought of that particular expense caused Basil to rally smartly.

'Lead on Dr. Huxley. I am intrigued to see how you propose to play God in this your land of the living dead; the dead- all of them akin to our old friend Lazarus.'

He waited for a response but Charles, satisfied that his ruse had had the desired effect only smiled, though somewhat grimly and led on. They were taken through two more rooms, offices where young ladies operated computers with nimble fingers and answered telephones which seemed to ring more often than Basil cared to see. At the end of a long corridor they arrived at a heavy metal door in which a large double glazed window had been set.

'Here we are Sir Basil,' said Charles, 'if you will step up here to the window I will switch on the lights to allow you to view the storage units. I'm afraid we cannot enter- heat from the environment causes some of the liquid nitrogen to vaporise and though we top up the dewars on a constant basis we do not want to cause unnecessary vaporization.'

'Far be it for me to cause you needless expense Dr. Huxley.' Said Basil. As he moved towards the window Charles pulled a switch and the room behind the glass was instantly flooded with lights. Almost as in his nightmare Basil saw the huge storage units in their jar-free cradles reflecting slivers of light from their metallic surfaces like a series of bizarre Christmas trees. Gently, imperceptibly they were moving, thought Basil these glittering monsters were themselves alive and breathing. It could have been a scene from Dante's inferno- an Antarctic inferno. A noise like the buzzing of a thousand bees could be heard issuing from behind the door providing a kind of eerie counterpoint. 'The noise- I suppose that is the refrigeration unit?' 'We have no refrigeration unit, Sir Basil' said Charles. 'Liquid nitrogen is the only freezing unit we require and is readily available in cylinders from many suppliers. The noise you hear is the topping up of the dewars which happens on a routine basis. In this way suspension is cheap and above all reliable. We are not, I am happy to be able to tell you, at the mercy of any power failures.'

Basil was impressed- more, he was intimidated by the horrible spectacle. He was again, as in his dream, reduced to be an unnatural silence.

Clarissa felt a renewed twinge of pity for him. She realised that to be confronted by the immensity of the project had not been on his agenda. Basil had come to London prepared to ridicule to mock and to laugh the project to scorn. He had meant to treat Immortality Inc. and Charles Huxley with contempt. The picture, in full colour as it were, the visible reality, had beaten him. He could see for himself that people actually put good money down to be frozen. Deranged people.

'Waiting room for the future,' he remarked lamely and followed Charles and Clarissa back to the office. It hit him then, that this game he thought Clarissa had been playing was not a game at all. It was real. Here was a flourishing concern in which she was heavily involved. Heavily financially involved. To stop her now would require more than words, more than ridicule. He began to be afraid. 'Well now Basil,' said Clarissa, 'I see that you are impressed. Are you going to sign on?' 'Certainly not. One potential lunatic in the family is quite enough. Though to be fair Dr. Huxley I must congratulate you. This enterprise is clearly well set up and I hope, making a huge profit . Is that the case?'

'A modest profit at the moment Sir Basil. But we expect to realise greater profits in the not too distant future.'

How distant is that future? I am sure you can understand my concern Dr. Huxley.'

'Indeed I do appreciate your concern Sir Basil, and when we have firm figures from our accounts department I will let you know.' Charles sidestepped the question he had no intention of answering.

'And now a cup of tea everyone?' One of the girls in the outside office brought in a tray prepared earlier. Clarissa poured and Charles offered a plate containing small squares of what in appearance were like thick pieces cur from a chocolate cake.

'Will you have one of these Sir Basil- they are a kind of cookie made by my Mom- chocolate brownies- she sent them over from San Francisco for me, knowing how much I like them.'

'Goodness Hux, all the way from San Francisco?' Clarissa was surprised. Basil took one saying, 'A food parcel from the bereft America no less.' He and Clarissa exchanged a bemused glance which Charles fortunately failed to see. Basil bit into the confection and chewed. The taste was sweet and chocolatey. Too sweet, too soggy and the nuts in the mixture were leathery and stuck in his teeth. 'Delicious,' lied Clarissa also chewing laboriously. They washed down (literally) the mixture with tea and refused a second square. Clarissa swiftly changed the subject. 'Will you join us for dinner Basil or have you made other arrangements?' 'I'm driving back to the Hall Clarissa. No point in hanging about in this polluted atmosphere.' 'Please yourself Basil.'

'Now Clarissa, I need to know, will we have the pleasure of your company this weekend?' Charles observed happily that Basil's question was tantamount to a plea. 'Perhaps I will Basil, I haven't decided yet.'

'You do remember that Rupert is bringing the pony over on the weekend- I'd like you to have a look at it.' He was definitely begging now noted Charles. Clarissa hesitated for a moment and then replied, 'In that case Basil, I will certainly be there.' Charles' face showed his displeasure and Clarissa was quick to reassure him, 'don't worry Hux you will manage very well without me. Since Zil has decided to lash out on another pony for the girls, a rare occurrence Hux, one I never thought I would ever live to see, I must be there to help.'

'I'm so glad Clarissa,' but Basil's face did not reflect his expressed joy. He shook his head gloomily and continued, 'The fact that Zil is being overly extravagant is neither here nor there; the way things are going,' he looked significantly at Charles and Clarissa, 'I'm afraid the Hall will simply collapse around or ears.' Clarissa smiled but Charles saw her concern. 'That's quite enough Basil- go home. I'll see you on Friday night.' Charles took Basil to the door, bade him farewell relieved to see the back of him and returned to Clarissa with a grave face. Basil in pathetic mien, Basil requiring sympathy was a real threat. He would retaliate immediately. 'Clarissa...' he said taking her hand, '...my very dear Clarissa, I have important news. There is something I must tell you; the powers that be at head office in the U.S. are making noises about replacing me here in London, now that we're up and running and making such a tidy profit. The rumour mill tells me that the next location for me may be Australia.' Clarissa paled, 'Australia- but that is in the middle of nowhere- I mean it is nowhere. It's thousands and thousand of miles away, and Hux there's nothing there.'

'Don't be silly Clarissa, of course there is- there's weather, good weather I mean...oh... lots of things. That famous Opera house for one.'

'As far as I know that's all there is- I see glimpses of the country when Mrs. Jenkins watches those dreary Australian soaps on television and I tell you Hux it looks awful- all that sea and sand and tropical heat- I'm sure it's the most ghastly place- not to mention those frightful accents- worse even than the Americans...I mean...'

She stopped, mortified. Charles laughed, 'Enough Clarissa, enough, please don't upset yourself. The move is not imminent, but I felt obliged to warn you that there are rumblings.' He put his arms around her and found she was trembling.

'It's not only Australia Hux- it's realisation that you're pushing me, that's it isn't it, am I right?' Charles replied gently, 'Yes Clarissa, that is exactly my intention. Time is running out for us.' Clarissa felt the familiar stirring of guilt mixed with a new fear- this time of the future. She rested her head on Charles' shoulder and could not find a reply.

CHAPTER TWENTY-TWO

To awake to the spectacle of Basil bearing a laden tea tray was an unnerving experience. Clarissa rubbed her eyes and rose on one elbow, 'What is it Basil- what happened- what's wrong?' 'Nothing is wrong Clarissa,' Basil said wounded, 'I am merely bringing you a cup of tea in bed. I realise that you have had a hard week and I thought this would be my charitable deed for the day. Sit up and I will pour.'

Entirely nonplussed Clarissa sat up. Basil plumped the pillows behind her.

'It's a beautiful day my dear. Now after you've had your tea I want you to dress quickly. Steve is making breakfast for us and after that we will walk down to the far paddock to have a look at the pony, Rupert said he'd be here at about ten.' He handed Clarissa her cup.

'Steve still around then Basil?' Basil knew that his best effort had misfired. He could kick himself. However, Steve was still around and very visible so what the hell. He would brazen it out. 'I have been too busy to find another career and especially one who will put with Mother's peccadillos. Be fair Clarissa, Steve is so wonderfully patient with mother she is irreplaceable just now.' Clarissa only smiled like the Giaconda and sipped her tea. Thank you for this thoughtful gesture Basil- the tea is absolutely delicious. Tell Steve I'll be down n a minute to sample her breakfast.' Basil crushed, made his way downstairs. Remobilisation was in order. After the trip to London, which has so thoroughly opened his eyes, Basil had decided the time had come to change his tactics. His intention was to be particularly nice to Clarissa so that she would be, not only morally obliged to him but fastened firmly to him and to the Hall. He accepted that the first act of his drama had fizzled badly, but the whole weekend was still before him. Optimism an unlikely sensation for the pessimistic and cynical Basil, filled his breast. Unaware of the playlet being enacted upstairs, Steve happily grilled bacon. She was perfectly content with her life at the Gate House and accepting of the part she was required to play. She had no designs on Basil other than to continue to join in his sexual games which she found intriguing and satisfying. Moreover she was equally at ease with Clarissa present or absent. She liked Clarissa and admired her stoicism. She believed without question Basil's tales of his relationship with his frigid wife and accepted these as justification for his infidelities. Steve, like many young women, was not burdened by guilt, neither did she blame. She lived in the moment. Further than today she did not speculate.

After a hearty and uneventful breakfast, Clarissa and Basil walked together down to the far paddock. The sky was cloudless and clear, the day promised to be one of those perfect English summer days that happen sometimes in August. The sparkling sunshine flooding the green fields delighted and at the same time saddened Clarissa. Because Hux was not here to share this unusually glorious weather with her. His visits here had been on dull, grey; he had never seen the Hall and its grounds at their best.

'What are you thinking Clarissa?'

'Nothing much Basil- only that this day is so beautiful...' Recklessly Basil plunged, 'I've missed you Clarissa, missed you badly. Life at the Hall is not the same without you here and I'm...well... I admit it, lonely. The house seems so empty when you are away. I wish you would spend more time here- more time with me.'

This speech, diffidently made by an uncommonly subdued Basil, bewildered Clarissa. It sounded rehearsed but in there somewhere she detected a grain of sincerity. 'Don't make me feel guilty Basil- I suspect that you are quite happy here without me- and I haven't forgotten that you have Steve here to fill those rare, lonely moments.'

Basil bit his lip in frustration. A rebuttal did not spring quickly to mind. Clarissa was spared further intimate revelations, none of which she wanted to hear from this despondent and almost woebegone Basil, by the sight of three small figures running towards them. The girls, dressed for riding hurled themselves joyfully into her arms. 'The pony is here- look Clarissa look, isn't she gorgeous?' With Zil and Teresa in the audience the examination of the pony began. Rupert led the small, white mare around in a circle, first walking, then trotting. She was 13 hands high, delicately made, with slender legs and tiny hoofs. 'She looks like a real lady,' said Clarissa 'I like her. What about temperament Rupert is she easy to handle?' 'Foolproof Clarissa. She's 14 years old- my children have all learnt to ride on her. She has a soft mouth and lovely manners I assure you.' Harriet was jumping up and down with excitement. 'Her name is snowflake Clarissa, isn't that just perfect- please now can I ride her Daddy please, please?' 'What do you think Rupert?' asked Zil. 'Saddle her up Zil- she'll be no problem for Harry, I've seen how she rides. Didn't you win a ribbon at the gymkhana Harry, in your riding Class?'

'I got a red one- second,' said Harriet proudly.

'Now remember girls,' Rupert addressed them gravely, 'you will have to keep snowflake very clean. A white horse needs lots of washing and brushing.'

'We promise, we promise...' the girls full of righteous zeal, all spoke at once, promising to wash and brush Snowflake every day and night. As the men began to saddle Snowflake, Teresa drew Clarissa aside. 'I've something to tell you Clarissa...' Teresa spoke very quietly, '...I'm pregnant.' 'Oh darling what good news- I suspect as much.' 'How did you know?' asked Teresa, disappointed that Clarissa was not more surprised. 'Those big shirts didn't fool me Teresa. But congratulations my darling- that really is good news. Is Zil pleased?' 'He doesn't know yet- in the meantime I've continued to keep him on the cold baths, herbal drinks and horseradish routine.' Clarissa burst into peals of laughter. 'Teresa that is priceless- my poor son, finally bearing at least some of the discomforts of pregnancy.' Teresa laughing too said, 'But I will tell him tonight- pay-back time is over. Though I must tell you it was fun while it lasted.' 'Did you follow the instructions to the letter?'

'To the letter Clarissa. If we have a son all the credit will be yours.' 'Nonsense Teresa- I still think the chances of a boy or girl are fifty-fifty no matter what elaborate methods are employed. When is the baby due?'

'In about three months- round about the time of your birthday- like last time.'

'Let's hope the outcome is not the same. But now let's watch Harry. I do hope Zil will buy Snowflake for the girls- they really do need another pony.'

As Clarissa watched the brushing of the pony- by Eddie, then saddling- by Zil, the bridling- by Basil, watching their darks heads close together, engrossed in their tasks she suddenly had no doubt that they no longer needed her. The feeling was strong- perhaps now she could leave them. Perhaps this was the sign.

The day continued blue and hot. Small white puff balls of clouds hung in the sky as though some distant Indian was sending up smoke signals. Swallows swooped low over the lawns searching for insects with which to feed their young. The gardens shone as though freshly polished by the sun while Clarissa continued to be wooed by Basil. Elizabeth and Steve had been banished to the village to call on the Vicar and his wife Hermione who was momentarily in a lucid, on-the-wagon phase. Basil and Clarissa were alone. Basil took Clarissa by the hand and led her to the walled garden where sweet-smelling jasmine climbed, where the rambling roses tumbled and dropped their petals on the green lawn. Between the well-laid paths, alyssum and thyme and phlox bloomed and scented the air. A picnic had been devised by the thoughtful new Basil. He had laid it out prettily on a table set under a green and white striped umbrella- the champagne in an ice bucket, the smoked salmon, the cold chicken, the salads and a fresh, crusty loaf. 'Have you been ordering from Harrods Basil?' A good deal of thought had clearly gone into the planning of this weekend. Basil nodded.

'An expensive exercise surely?'

'Nothing is too good for you Clarissa,' said Basil ignoring Clarissa's skeptical moue and pouring champagne into her glass. I propose a toast, to my loving and well-loved wife.'

Clarissa took the glass and drank- bemused she drank again. This was a calculated and banal effort on Basil's part to win her back, to separate her from Hux- so much was obvious. She was reminded of the callow youth he had once been, heavy-handedly planning seduction. And yet to watch as he clumsily placed smoke salmon on her plate, broke bread and offered it to her as though she was truly his cherished, his beloved wife, cut her to the heart. This pragmatic, sardonic Englishman was humbling himself in his massive efforts to please. Despite herself she remembered again their early days together, when his attentions his courting of her had been genuine. She checked the thought- possibly he had not been honest even then. His counterfeit affection, in the beginning even manifesting itself as passion, which had been second nature in those early days, he had abandoned long ago and was with some difficulty recalling now. Clarissa wanted to stop- she was embarrassed; she wanted to restore him to his usual, brutally sarcastic self. She was no longer able to watch his bizarre behaviour with equanimity and worse, was unable to respond to it. Her confusion was complete. She sipped her champagne in silence, avoiding his eyes, wondering desperately how to put a halt to this sentimental onslaught. 'Tell me Clarissa do you remember the day when we became engaged, when you and I...' Clarissa, desperate now, interrupted, 'This is really a delightful picnic Basil...' she took a deep breath- the solution had come to her as if dispensed by a heavenly hand, '...you know I've been meaning to tell you something which may make you very happy.' Basil's expression changed from slightly anxious to complacent. He had known all along that it wouldn't take much to turn matters around when he put his mind to it. Silently he congratulated himself. 'Yes my dear?' Already his tone had become patronising. Clarissa's relief echoed in her strengthening voice. 'I have decided Basil...'she held out her glass for a refill of champagne, 'I have decided that it will not be necessary for me to apply for a full body suspension...' Basil smiled, preparing to accept, of course graciously, the surrender he felt certain was on her lips.

'...Yes Basil- I have decided that it will only be necessary to freeze my head. After my death, before the whole body is frozen they will cut off my head and maintain it in the cryocapsule, a smaller one of course, rather than suspending the complete body, which after the beheading will simply be discarded. This latest process is called neuro-suspension. It is quite a large step forward in the field of cryonics.' Basil's face had darkened increasingly during Clarissa's rapid speech. His demeanour became almost threatening. Clarissa's timid smile was meant to be placatory.

'I do hope you are pleased?' Basil found his voice. 'What...' he shouted '... what the hell do you mean?' 'I mean exactly what I said- neuro-suspension, the freezing of my head alone-is now my preferred option. I will not have my whole body frozen. I thought you would be thrilled to hear that.' 'Thrilled?...Are...are...you quite...mad?' Basil had become virtually incoherent, 'No Basil,' Clarissa bravely maintained her matter-of-fact tone. 'Neuro-suspension is a perfectly acceptable method of employing the cryogenic process.' Basil's voice returned, amplified.

'But what will you do when you are defrosted? That is if you are defrosted, which is of course totally unlikely. You will have no body to go with your head- you will be nothing more than an exhibit in a freak show.'

'Oh no I won't. The solution to that minor problem is ridiculously easy. They will simply clone my body back for me. A younger, much stronger and much healthier body.' 'You have completely taken leave of your senses Clarissa- I am shocked to the core with your...your relentless obsession with all of this foolishness.' 'But Basil my poor darling do calm down. Think of what this means. Neuro-suspension is not as expensive as full body suspension. I must admit the cost will be almost as much but it will not be quite the huge sum you have been expecting.' 'And that is your latest and most maniacal decision?'

But behind those familiar blue eyes, looking so defiantly at him, Basil noted there lurked a doubt.

CHAPTER TWENTY-THREE

The notice fastened to the wall beneath a portrait of an early Basil Hare Bell, (the full and straggly grey beard bearing witness to a stately Victorian Hare Bell) was not only incongruous, it disrupted the historic atmosphere of the Hall.

EMERGENCY PROCEDURES IN CASE OF DEATH- it read in large, red capital letters. Were one to approach more closely, the smaller type (in black lower case) could be easily deciphered, were one in the least interested in the many paragraphs guaranteed to enumerate the most offensive of physical details.

At the table below this alien intrusion onto the historic walls of the Hall, the celebration of Clarissa's birthday was in progress. Preparations for this auspicious event had been in train for some weeks. Teresa had devised the menu at her cooking class. These culinary lessons- a suggestion of Zil's she had taken to heart, had been extensive and comprehensive. What's more she had enjoyed the whole exercise. After this, her ultimate pregnancy, she planned to sack Cook, an event which she was looking forward with some pleasure. Canny cook had already seen the writing on the wall and while not having actually given notice (another position with her credentials could in these modern times be difficult to find) she had become recalcitrant and stubborn, allowing Teresa only limited access to her kitchen. She was not in the least impressed by the fact Teresa had discovered garlic. On the contrary- she maintained that it was a powerful poison guaranteed to kill the family, and that, slowly. It was fortunate that during the week preceding Clarissa's birthday, Cook ailing mother had once again succumbed to an obscure disease which required her daughter's presence. Teresa seized the moment. Her newly acquired skills were to be put to the test.

Basil, at the head of the table, was in spirits so low that even his usually joyfully abundant hair drooped and clung unhappily close to his skull. He looked miserable. Clarissa was still playing her double game, much as he was used to playing it and she was playing it depressingly well. He was in constant receipt of his own medicine which tasted more than bitter, indeed it was threatening to choke him. Despite his best efforts to entice her back to his hearth she was evading decisions, dangling him on a string like an animated and impotent puppet. He was being cleverly manipulated and was quite unable to think of any further and ultimately victorious moves to win this most serious of games.

Clarissa over the past many months had been on the see-saw of decision-making. Her inconsistency of rational thought, her lack of commitment to weighty cogitation, her continuing procrastination a further ineffectiveness, all these she had borne with a measure of remarkable irresponsibility, but now she accepted that her incapacity had reached its zenith. A resolution was not only overdue it would finally be achieved. In short, Clarissa's mind had finally been made up. There had at least been steps in the right direction. Plans were afoot and in motion. In this frame of mind her demeanour was light-hearted and festive. Her mood was reflected in her face which tonight caused her to look particularly beautiful. She was relaxed and determined to enjoy her birthday celebrations.

Steve was sitting beside an Elizabeth dressed for the celebration as Diamond Lil. She was wearing a slinky, diamonte studded number in electric blue satin. On her grey head a diamond tiara flashed and sparkled. It was a head-piece Basil had not seen before. He wondered for a brief and optimistic moment whether the diamonds were real then dismissed the thoughts as wishful thinking. Mrs. Jenkins, who was helping Teresa in the kitchen but only on this one special occasion, as she had made perfectly plain, brought in the first course, a mushroom soup. Without her feather duster she looked positively naked though her huge golden hoop earrings caught the light and twinkled as she moved, easily making up for the duster deficiency. 'And where,' asked Basil, 'is the ubiquitous Dr. Huxley tonight Clarissa?' He did not appear to be at all distressed at the lack of Dr. Huxley at the birthday table. Clarissa explained, 'Poor Hux, circumstances conspired against him all day but he will be here later I hope- probably after dinner.' 'Such a pity,' said Zil 'I did want him to be here for Teresa's debut as cook extraordinaire. This soup is delicious my darling.'

'That recipe is from a very early lesson Zil- but wait till you taste my piece de resistance- coq-au-vin.'

'Teresa, I agree wholeheartedly with Zil,' said Basil, 'you have excelled yourself with the soup. I am most impressed and especially tonight since I'm sure you've been standing in the kitchen for hours which must have been quite arduous for you in your interesting condition.'

'Thank you Basil but I must tell you that my condition hardly bothers me I've become so accustomed to it. How to cope with not being pregnant will be the problem. I see it as a challenge- a condition so entirely new and wonderful that somehow I don't think it will take me very long to master. It will be a truly interesting condition.' 'And what exactly were the circumstances that conspired against poor Hux tonight?' asked Zil. Clarissa began, 'First of all he had an extremely heated exchange with the relative of two of our latest suspensees...' 'Two in one family,' interrupted Basil, at the mention of Charles Huxley he was recovering his irony, 'I would say that's overdoing it...' 'It was a husband and wife- in a car crash. Their son demanded a discount since it was for the two at once.' 'Just like boarding school,' said Basil 'did he get the discount?'

'Of course not. Hux was obliged to explain that the upkeep costs exactly the same for the maintenance of each separate suspensee.'

'Good old Hux- he's tough when it matters. Still I suppose you can't run a business on charity. It's the poor son I feel sorry for- two on ice- that expense boggles the mind.'

'It's Hux I feel for Basil. After that debacle Cynthia left the office in hysterics because even with her supposed skills she had not been able to hose the situation down. Hux was quite displeased with her...'

'So would I have been,' said Basil 'those do-gooding counselling people need help more often than your disturbed clients it seems to me. Sack her I say.' 'Who's being tough now Basil? Cynthia has her uses, few though they may be.' Clarissa too had found Cynthia and her holier-than-thou posturing attitudes rather hard to bear. Fundamentally she agreed with Basil.

Then Mrs. Jenkins, a delicious aroma wafted ahead of her brought the coq-au-vin to the table. The dispatching of this succulent stew reduced the table to a temporary silence. Diamond Lil was the first to speak.

'The curve,' she said thoughtfully, 'is more powerful than the sword.' Everyone laughed, and Elizabeth smiled with them. She had obtained their attention- a universal trait to be found without exception in children, actors and the totally self-obsessed.

'Congratulations Teresa' said Clarissa 'the cooking classes are a tremendous success. You'll have to teach me- I can't produce anything as good as this.'

'It's not difficult really Clarissa- after this baby arrives I intent to go on and do the honours course- to learn how to cook really exotic dishes. This dish is basically terribly old-fashioned.'

'But delicious.' Said Zil.

'I do miss that American gentleman,' said Elizabeth, 'now there was a man who appreciated me and my art. Where is he?'

'I miss him too Elizabeth,' said Clarissa with a quick glance at Basil 'but he has had such a difficult day. I haven't told you all about the real disaster that occurred today- you won't believe it but they discovered a leak in one of the cryocapsules- imagine that.' 'Good heaven's said Basil with a smirk, 'what a calamity- is the crycapsule occupied?'

'Of course it is. Don't laugh Basil it can be a very serious problem. You see the liquid nitrogen simply leaks into the air, vaporises invisibly and the flask slowly empties. The body began to thaw and I needn't describe the consequences- they can be very bad indeed.'

'Bad?' I would say rotten and very quickly too. Remember when Zil used the freezer power point for his electric drill and forgot to plug the freezer back in? The smell of rotting food had permeated the whole house by the time we discovered the problem and then cleaned the whole freezer out. We couldn't get rid of the smell for weeks.'

'Stop it Basil- you'll make Teresa sick even at this late stage in her pregnancy.'

'But the leak?' asked Zil 'is it stoppable? And how was it discovered?'

'We have an alarm system- when the level of liquid nitrogen drops to a certain level it sounds and alerts the duty engineer. And so no harm done since the suspensees are in fact suspended upside down- for obvious reasons.'

'You mean so that the brain remains frozen no matter what?' 'Yes Zil,' he continued, 'Your 'no matter what' being a euphemism for the fact that the feet begin to deteriorate- in fact to rot?' Clarissa, caught out, began hesitantly, 'But that doesn't really matter because...' Basil laughing loudly broke in, 'Gives an entirely new meaning to the word 'foot-rot,' 'stop it Basil, it's my birthday and caustic remarks are not permitted tonight.' Basil subsided, satisfied that he had scored yet another point.

'Are we all finished?' Not waiting for a reply Teresa rang the small brass bell on the table before her to summon Mrs. Jenkins who arrived at a trot. 'You could clear now Mrs. Jenkins and I think we are ready for the cake.'

'Not waiting for Hux, Teresa?' asked Clarissa anxiously, 'He'll be here quite soon I'm sure.'

'No point waiting Clarissa,' Teresa bent towards her and whispered, 'we must get Elizabeth put to bed. With all this unaccustomed excitement she may become violent. Remember what happened at the vicarage tea party last year?' Clarissa nodded, unhappily in agreement.

CHAPTER TWENTY-FOUR

Mrs. Jenkins came in from the kitchen carrying a large brown cake topped with an inch of flesh pink icing and alight with many small red and purple candles. She placed it carefully in front of Clarissa. In the candlelight her golden earrings shook and dazzled the eyes of the company. 'Here we are m'lady- a happy birthday to you. Isn't it a pretty cake? One of Mrs. Paynes best efforts- her famous chocolate mud cake.' Elizabeth clapped her hands, 'Oh how lovely- a beautiful cake with pink icing, my favourite colour. I want to blow out the candles.' 'No Gran,' said Teresa firmly 'you can't- it's not your birthday- its Clarissa's.'

'It always seems to be Clarissa's birthday. Why can't I have a birthday too?'

'You no longer have birthdays mother, remember? It was entirely your own choice, no one compelled you to give up these annual celebrations.' Basil attempted to remonstrate, unsuccessfully as it turned out.

'Well I've just changed my mind.' Like a small child frustrated in its immediate desire, Elizabeth began to chant loudly, 'I want a birthday- I want a birthday- make me a birthday tomorrow Basil, with a cake and lots of candles and pink icing and everything .'

'Oh dear,' said Steve 'she's becoming more impossible every day. I hardly know what to do with her.'

'Ask Clarissa,' said Basil spitefully, 'she seems to have all the answers.'

'Why ask me?' replied Clarissa 'she's your mother Basil.' 'I am not a Mother' said Elizabeth, 'I am Mae West- ask anyone- ask that nice American Man. I am the famous Mae West. I have the same dimensions as the Venus de Milo but I've got it on her- I've got two whole arms and what's more I know how to use them...' she threw out the said arms triumphantly and added, '...and what more I'm not marble!'

'Dear Elizabeth,' said Clarissa, 'she demands and needs attention- just like the rest of us.' Thus encouraged Elizabeth continued, 'That's true Clarissa. Why does no one ever think about me, about my life, about my achievements. No one ever gives me credit. All you people ever trouble your heads about is yourselves- all you ever think about are your own miserable strivings. The older people grow the more they become concerned with themselves. With themselves alone and of course with survival. They struggle for their own survival at all costs. The young don't bother, they know they cannot die, that they will never die- they recognise that only the old die. And I, being the famous Mae West will never die.' This unusual outburst silenced the company for a moment- some recognised themselves and were briefly ashamed. Basil attempted to pacify the overwrought Elizabeth. 'Mother you are absolutely right- the young, they are the future. That's the secret and you have discovered it- do not grow old- remain young.' Clarissa quickly responded, 'or be remade young- that is what I will do. I am quite amazed Basil that at last you see some logic in my so-called crazy scheme.'

'Not a bit of it Clarissa, I was merely agreeing with Mother's sentiments. You know my views. While I most certainly do believe that the future belongs to the young I do not believe that this same future will be directed by the rotting, thawed out bodies of diseased old fossils with their rigid, conservative views. The young will have no use for any of you. There's no turning the clock back Clarissa, no matter how hard you try.'

'Fortunately Basil I am more optimistic than you with your cynical attitudes. I say let the future take care of itself; I am prepared to take my chances there.'

'So your decision is quite final on that point Clarissa, your body or perhaps your head will definitely be frozen?' 'Probably Basil, I haven't actually signed up yet but I intend to do so very soon.' 'Clarissa these candles are guttering,' said Teresa, 'do blow them out before they melt the cake entirely.' 'Of course darling, musn't ruin Mrs. Payne's fantastic mud cake.' Clarissa took a deep breath and blew with gusto. 'There- all out at once.' She put her hand to her heart puffing a little and clearly breathless. 'Whew- that was quite and effort.' Leaning heavily back in her chair, Clarissa took her hand from her heart and put it to her forehead, 'Goodness me- I feel quite dizzy…' Basil said at once,

'Take another deep breath Clarissa- it's only a reaction to the blowing out of the candles- that kind of unaccustomed activity always makes one feel a trifle dizzy but it will only be for a moment.'

'What did you wish this time mother?' asked Zil. 'That's my secret Zil…oh dear… but I really do feel funny…I seem to have a pain- right here…' Again Clarissa's hand went to her heart. Concerned now Zil asked, 'Mother, mother- are you alright?' 'Oh yes… I think so but…' This time Clarissa doubled up, obviously in agony. Basil ran to her as she slipped off her chair and collapsed onto the Persian rug. She lay there, faced up, quite still.

'Clarissa…Clarissa…oh my God…she's fainted.'

Steve was the first to move-she ran to find a pillow and placed it under Clarissa's head. Zil, Basil and even the bulky Teresa knelt beside the inert figure, patted the limp hands and place face without immediate result. Then Mrs. Jenkins, apparently having heard the commotion, hurried in and quietly and purposefully took over.

'Now just a minute everyone, stand back; stand back give her air- lots of air...she'll rally in a minute.' She knelt at Clarissa's side, loosened her clothing and in a professional manner took Clarissa's wrist in her hand. The onlookers stood motionless, white-faced and helpless, gazing hopefully at Mrs. Jenkins' ministrations.

'What are you doing Mrs. Jenkins- will she be alright...?' 'I'm just taking her pulse Sir Basil. Now don't you worry yourself, I know all about first aid- the St. John Ambulance you know. We're on duty all the time- football, cricket, any entertainment where there's likely to be an injury and God knows that takes in just about everything you can think of these days.' She continued proudly, 'As well as that I'm a pink lady at the cottage hospital. I can tell you that you learn a lot by just watching what goes on with those doctors and nurses' 'But what is it Mrs. Jenkins, what on earth is wrong with her? She was perfectly fine one minute and the next...' Basil was distraught. Steve bent down and tried to raise Clarissa's head. Mrs. Jenkins waved her away, 'leave her alone, don't touch her- I'm sure it's nothing, just a funny turn, my Gran did it every Sunday before church, regularly as clockwork.'

'But she's unconscious,' said Basil, 'she's not coming to, what shall we do...? Mrs. Jenkins still officiously taking Clarissa's pulse now put her head to Clarissa's chest. She listened for a long moment. At last she looked hopelessly at Basil. 'Uh dear...oh dear... oh dear' 'What is it woman- what's the matter- speak up...' 'Oh my goodness Sir Basil- I'm afraid she's gone.' 'Gone...gone?...what are you saying?' 'Gone Sir Basil- expired as they say.' 'But that can't be...not so quickly...' 'I'm afraid it's really true Sir Basil- she's dead. Dead as a door nail.' Teresa burst into tears 'Oh no- it can't be- not Clarissa, oh how awful...' 'It's not possible,' said Basil, 'she can't die, not just like that.' Mrs. Jenkins sat back on her heels. 'She's dead alright- I've seen too many dead bodies not to be certain. They often go suddenly like that- heart attack I'll be bound.' She took Clarissa's hands and folded them across her Chest. Zil suddenly galvanised, ran to his mother's side.

'It can't be- there must be something we can do to revive her.' He moved forward but Mrs. Jenkins placed herself squarely in front of Clarissa's body.

'It's no use Master Zil, no use at all. I've seen lots of them go like that and when they're gone they're gone. Nothing you can do about it- nothing anyone can do.'

Zil sat on the floor beside his mother, head in his hands. 'How awful, how ghastly to die like that- blowing out the candles on her birthday cake - how horribly iconic.'

'Oh...oh...poor Clarissa...I can't believe it...' cried Teresa, a handkerchief to her face mopping up the tears that ran freely. Elizabeth, still at the table and unperturbed by the drama taking place around her was sticking her fingers in the pink icing on the cake and then licking them clean with obvious relish

'Well then,' Said Mrs. Jenkins briskly, 'I'll just call the mobile emergency van.' She went to the notice hanging on the wall below the portrait of the ancient Victorian Hare Bell and read aloud, 'Emergency procedures in case of death. First of all, that will be Step one- call the mobile van, fully equipped with heart lung machine- this can be done by dialling 51234...' Basil interrupted, 'No- wait Mrs. Jenkins, do not telephone- I refuse to have that obscene vehicle on my property.' Mrs. Jenkins did not immediately obey.

'But Sir Basil, whatever do you mean- it's what she said she wanted.' 'She's my wife- I will decide how to...how to...dispose of her...of her...body.'

'But Sir Basil- she talked about cryo-what's its name all the time- frozen I'll be, she said...'

'No- she is my wife- I forbid it.' Mrs. Jenkins courageously continued to argue.

'But Sir Basil you must do it- she'd set her heart on being frozen. And there's no time to be lost- we must summon the van immediately,' she continued to read from the emergency notice, 'Step two- within moments of death the body must be attached to a heart lung machine to maintain the circulation of the blood in order to prevent the brain and other vital organs from deteriorating." All that special equipment is in the van- I'm going to phone for it.' She moved towards the telephone on a side table and began to dial. Basil followed her and broke the connection. 'Just a minute Mrs. Jenkins- not so fast- let me think...' 'Father,' said Zil urgently, 'Mrs. Jenkins is right. We must respect Mother's wishes- let her call the van.' 'No Zil, your mother had not made that final decision to be frozen- she was still vacillating. You all heard her not ten minutes ago. She had not signed up. In these circumstances I will make the decision for her. As her husband, I say let's leave her undisturbed. She should have a normal, Christian burial.' Through her tears Teresa said, 'No Basil- Clarissa's wish and intention was to be frozen- you know that as well as we all do'

'I agree with Teresa.' Said Zil 'let's call the van.' Furiously Basil said, 'How can you two say that? We were all agreed that cryonics is a crazy idea. And Zil, what about the Hall? If we freeze her the maintenance of her body will ruin us. I say let's bury her in the family plot. That's where she belongs.' 'No Basil –you are playing God. I insist that we carry out Clarissa's last wishes no matter what it costs.' 'Teresa, please be reasonable. I am not playing God I am merely making the correct, the sensible decision.'

On the deep red Persian rug the body of Clarissa lay, motionless, forgotten in the heat of the argument. At the table Elizabeth having demolished half the pink icing began on the cake itself. Teresa began to cry again. Through her tears she sobbed, 'How can you go against her express wishes Basil- you cannot deny her- if you do refuse to freeze her how will you be able to live with yourself? You will feel guilty for the rest of your life.' Basil retorted quickly, 'Clarissa was not herself when she embraced that foolishness Teresa, that cryonics madness. She was unduly influenced by that…that Yank. She would have to come to her senses in the end I'm sure of it.' 'I don't think so Basil- in any case you seem to have forgotten something- it's Clarissa's money.'

'I know that Teresa but we must think of the cost to our descendants. We must take provision for them, for their future- we must not fail them.' Mrs. Jenkins made another move towards the telephone.

'Never mind the future Sir Basil- it's the here and now that matters. While you're all standing there arguing poor Lady Clarissa is deteriorating.'

'Is what?'

'Deteriorating- like it says here,' said Mrs. Jenkins indicating the emergency procedure notice. 'Deteriorating- going rotten. Many a time I've heard Dr. Hux say, remember Mrs. Jenkins (I've asked him to call me Rita but he can't bring himself to do it, he's a bit shy really) anyway, many's the time he said- remember Mrs. Jenkins, in case of a sudden death emergency, speed is of the essence. Now it says here- In the absence of the mobile van the following emergency procedure should be followed. 'Teresa moved to the telephone. Zil moved to prevent her, 'Don't do it Teresa- Father is right. I agree that mother should have a proper Christian burial.' 'I don't care what you two think, despite you both, I'm going to ring for the van.' Teresa dialled, listening for a moment and then threw the receiver down in disgust. 'It's engaged!' Mrs. Jenkins, untroubled by the arguments seething around her, continued to read aloud, 'Here it is- "The emergency procedure in the absence of the van is as follows. Wrap the body in aluminum foil and cover with ice." I can at least do that. The foil is in the pantry. Lady Clarissa saw to it that the cupboards here and at the Gate House were always kept fully stocked.' As she hurried off Teresa, avoiding Basil's eye, said quickly, 'Meanwhile I'll try the van again.' She dialed and once more found the number engaged. 'Damn!' She said and again slammed the receiver down. Mrs. Jenkins returned with several, extra wide rolls of Home Brand Aluminum foil and began clumsily to open the boxes and to extract the material within. Without any help from the others she began to wrap the shiny metallic sheets around Clarissa's lifeless body. 'Teresa,' said Basil 'I don't understand you- you are nothing but a hypocrite. Previously you were dead against cryonics in every shape and form. You maintained that it was unnatural, unchristian and revolting. Now suddenly you are supporting it wholeheartedly.' 'I am not supporting cryonics Basil, I am supporting Clarissa. It is far more important to respect the wishes of the dead than to go along with the selfish opinions of those in dissent.' Mrs. Jenkins wrestling with the foil as she wrapped the body of Clarissa became herself entangled in the shiny sheets which crackled and tore as she worked. Under her breath she was heard to mutter quiet imprecations. Basil ignoring Teresa's pleas said commandingly, 'Mrs. Jenkins that is a waste of time- stop it immediately. It's horrible to watch- its…it's obscene.' 'It's what she wanted Sir Basil. Now I need ice- Master Zil will you dash down to the village- there's an ice dispensing machine outside the off-license. I'll need at least four bags.' As Basil moved to prevent further wrapping from outside came the sound of a car driving up and stopping. A car door was heard to slam. Fearfully Mrs. Jenkins stopped her work and said, 'Oh dear, of dear- that will be Dr. Hux- my goodness me will he ever be upset!'

CHAPTER TWENTY-FIVE

The tableau that greeted Charles Huxley on his entrance into the Great Hall was a sight he would long remember. It was as though a multi-coloured medieval pageant had been painted by a master. In the centre, the table set for a festive occasion, crystal wine glasses glowing ruby with wine, ancient silver cutlery, crested and shining, Elizabeth in her place, her sapphire satin garment clinging to her body while her tiara glittered and gleamed and on the deep red Persian rug a strange figure, prone, covered all in silver like some medieval knight in armour. Nothing moved, only the tapestries hanging from the long walls swayed gently in the cold draught as was their wont. And there was Zil on his knees, Mrs. Jenkins cowering beside the armour-clad figure and Basil with his arm raised as though about to strike her while the heavily pregnant Teresa stood and sobbed loudly, as counterpoint to the only other sound breaking the silence of the magnificent room- his own footsteps echoing on the stone flags. And the absence of Clarissa- the ominous absence of his beloved Clarissa. Her family watched him as he approached. No one spoke or moved. Slowly a feeling of dread crept over him. He did not dare to speak, he did not dare to ask. Teresa's sobbing continued. At last through her tears she broke the unnatural silence and cried, 'It's so awful, so dreadful- it's like a nightmare- I wish I could wake up.' Mrs. Jenkins hoping to avoid explanations it was up to the family surely- began again to wrestle with the aluminium foil. But then her practical common sense prevailed. 'Ice Master Zil, we must have ice. Speed is of the essence in cases of sudden death.' In that single moment Charles Huxley saw and understood. He flung himself onto Clarissa's body, scattering aluminium foil and Mrs. Jenkins. 'It's not true, tell me it's not true, Clarissa, Clarissa, for God's sake- what happened here?' Mrs. Jenkins picked herself up and said calmly, 'Now watch yourself Dr. Hux or I'll have you wrapped up as well. I'm very sorry to tell you but Lady Clarissa has had a heart attack. She is dead. I'm following the instructions as per your emergency procedure notice A lot of ice is all we need now.'

'I can't believe it- she was so...so ...alive and now this. And I brought her a gift this time..for her birthday...' He broke down and sat beside Clarissa's body, mute, head in his hands. Teresa removed her handkerchief long enough to tell him, 'I've been trying to call the van Hux- the number appears to be engaged or possibly out of order. What should we do next?'

'The van?' asked Charles bemused, 'the can? What for?' 'To prepare Clarissa for suspension- you must remember that her wish is to be frozen?' Charles rose to his feet, 'No...no...' he almost shouted 'I won't let her go, I won't let her be frozen. I cannot do it to her...she was so warm, so alive, so...so warm...I cannot bear the thought of her suspended in a flask...all alone...in such icy coldness...' A Charles in his agony ran on, almost incoherently, Basil watched from the sidelines waiting for the tirade to cease. His moment soon arrived.

'I take it you agree with me then Dr. Huxley- there will be no suspension for my wife, no freezing- she will have a proper Christian burial after all?' Charles suddenly came to his senses; the significance of what Basil was saying hit him hard.

'I...I don't know- this has been so quick- you must give me time to think.' 'There's no time for that now Dr. Huxley- you know the process intimately. I believe quick action is required in these circumstances. From your reaction I deduce that deep down you do not want to freeze Clarissa any more than I do. Am I right?'

'Good God Sir Basil the decision is not mine to make. She is still your wife- you must decide. I simply do not know what to think. I'm too confused... I didn't realise that it would be like this... so ...so final. I want her back, warm and alive, not dead and frozen and suspended in a steel container; gone forever and no hope.' Ruthlessly Basil moved in for the kill. 'So you admit that the whole exercise is merely an expensive experiment. An experiment for others but not for your nearest and dearest?' Charles in total despair now nodded, 'Yes...yes you are right. I cannot bear the thought of walking into my warehouse knowing that she is there, suspended, frozen, dead.'

'So we are all agreed then- burial for Clarissa in the family plot?' Zil nodded.

'I don't care,' rejoined Charles heavy-hearted, 'what does it all matter now?'

'Poor, poor Clarissa,' said Teresa 'it's lucky that she will be forever unaware of her betrayal, your disloyalty, both of you. If only she could see how you have let her down.' 'But how did it happen?' Charles was still in denial. 'I can't believe that she is...' He broke down again. Zil replied sadly, 'she was blowing out the candles on her birthday cake and was overcome by a dizzy spell then suddenly collapsed. It must have been a heart attack.' From the table where she was still sitting, placidly chewing pieces of Clarissa's birthday cake, Elizabeth chimed in, 'If you had let me blow the candles none of this would have happened.'

'She could be right at that,' Said Mrs. Jenkins. 'I take it Sir Basil that you want me to stop the foil wrapping then?' 'Yes Mrs. Jenkins.'

Said Basil wearily, 'you may stop.' 'Poor Mother,' said Zil, 'and still so young. Let me see- she was only forty-nine.' 'No Zil you're wrong,' said Basil, 'I know she was at least fifty-six or even fifty-seven today.' Charles seemed surprised, 'That can't be right. She told me she was turning forty-two today.' Elizabeth spoke up. 'She never told me how old she was- but then nobody ever tells me anything.' 'Hux is right,' said Teresa 'I'm sure she was only forty-two today. She certainly didn't like fifty-seven Basil- that's ridiculous.' 'It's quite easy to work out,' said Basil 'Mother had me when she was eighteen, and I'm thirty-one which makes her forty-nine. There you are- I'm right.' Basil laughed, 'had you at eighteen, that's a nice fanciful little tale and you believed it?' 'Certainly I believe it- and I still believe it. She looks, I mean looked much younger than fifty-seven. Father I must agree with Teresa- fifty-seven is quite ridiculous.' Basil began to count on his fingers. 'Now let me see- I reckon she was at least twenty-five when you were born Zil- she might have been seventeen or eighteen when we became engaged...but no, there's no doubt about it- she's close to sixty.'

From the floor came sounds of foil tearing and the corpse of Clarissa rose up and came furiously to life. The visage of Lazarus had not so terrible an aspect. The corpse spoke. 'How dare you Basil- how dare you lie about my age- it's the very last straw- the ultimate perfidy.' Zil and Basil at first stunned were momentarily paralysed not only by her words but by her rage. They attempted to go to her but she waved them away as she tore the foil from her neck and arms. 'Mother- you're not dead...' wrathfully she continued, 'Obviously Zil. Only a fool, or two or three...' she looked contemptuously at all of them, 'would have accepted that I was. Not one of you made the slightest efforts to revive me or to call a doctor. I'd hate to have a real heart attack with you ignorant dolts in charge. I'd have no hope at all. It would be a complete disaster- in fact I'd be well and truly dead.' 'But Mrs. Jenkins was so...so...confident, so sure of her diagnosis,' protested Basil, 'She said you were dead and we believed her...' said Zil, 'If only I had been here,' Charles broke in self-righteously, 'I would have revived her.' 'Wise after the event...' Basil dismissed this lame justification, '...you, Dr. Huxley were not here to witness the incident.' Clarissa ignored them all, 'I must give Mrs. Jenkins her due- she did a marvellous job of convincing you of my demise.' Mrs. Jenkins simpered, and said smugly, 'I just did me best m'day,' 'nevertheless you others accepted her words with such alacrity that I began to wonder, from my uncomfortable position on the rug, whether you perhaps secretly wished me dead.'

They protested vehemently. Their arguments were delivered without conviction. Clarissa rose from the rug, dusted herself down and waited for the question which was yet to be voiced. The she moved to the table and saw the remains of her cake.

'In the meantime I'll have a piece of my birthday cake.'

'Me too, me too,' begged Elizabeth. Clarissa cut two slices, gave one to Elizabeth and began to eat her own piece. The sounds of munching were suddenly broken by Charles, Basil, Zil and Teresa all speaking at once, 'but why Clarissa? Why did you do it, why?' They clamoured in unison. 'At last,' said Clarissa, 'I thought you'd never ask. I did it to test you, to test your reactions and my God were they slow. That's the first discovery I made. I was tempted to let you stew a little longer but then your incomparable treachery Basil, roused me. You don't know how old I am any more than do the others- what's more I have no intention of revealing the exact date of my birth to any of you. You will all die wondering.'

'Thank God you're alive Clarissa,' said Charles, 'that's all that really matters.'

'Yes- of course I'm delighted too, that goes without saying.' Basil echoed hastily, 'few things in this world go without saying Basil- the tendency is for them to seize up instead. Teresa is the only one who need say nothing- the only one of you all who stood by me, stood by me so valiantly in the teeth of your combined opposition and despite her convictions. I will never forget it, Teresa- you are a woman of character and of great strength.' Clarissa embraced her. 'Thank you for those words Clarissa- after all we women must stick together...oh dear...' Teresa suddenly bit her lip and clutched her stomach, obviously in pain. Through clenched teeth she said, 'Oh no- here we go again. Zil- the baby is coming...' Automatically Basil took the phone and dialled while Zil ran to fetch the suitcase. 'Such a lot more I wanted to say Clarissa- sorry about the party- again,' Teresa managed a laugh through her pain. Zil returned with the case and embraced Clarissa. 'Mother I am so glad... so relieved that you're alright... you gave us a terrible fright- please don't ever do anything like that again.'

'Perhaps my sudden death and subsequent resurrection will give you food for thought Zil. But hurry now- we don't want the baby arriving on the Persian rug.' Hearing this Elizabeth disengaged herself from her piece of birthday cake. 'Not another baby- I can't believe it. Don't Teresa and Zil know where babies come from? I find it quite disgusting- just like rabbits.'

'She may well be right' said Teresa grimly as Basil and Zil helped her, pain-wracked but resigned to the car and thence to the cottage hospital.

Chapter Twenty-Five

Clarissa said meaningfully to Steve still sitting, entirely nonplussed by events, at the end of the table, 'Steve I think it's time for Elizabeth to go to bed don't you? I'm sure Mrs. Jenkins will drive you both back to the Gate House.' Mrs. Jenkins nodded, thankful to be released from this nights arduous obligations. 'Since I do feel a trifle weary,' said Elizabeth with dignity, 'I think perhaps I should retire. Thank you for the lovely party my dear Clarissa- so exciting- much more fun than the last one. You may escort me Steve.'

CHAPTER TWENTY-SIX

They arrived sometime later that same evening in the sitting room of the Gate House. Basil, Clarissa and Charles Huxley. Basil headed straight for the drinks cabinet. 'Anyone else?' he asked, pouring himself a large whiskey. They nodded. He poured two more which were accepted gratefully by Charles and Clarissa. Throwing himself into a chair Basil, seizing the initiative said, 'what a dirty

Trick Clarissa- how could you? What possessed you to give us all such a fright?' Clarissa did not reply, only sipped her whiskey. Basil mistaking her silence for acknowledgement of a guilt conscience continued piously, 'I never suspected that you were capable of such unscrupulous behaviour.' Clarissa came instantly to life. 'How dare you Basil! Don't you dare use the word unscrupulous to me, not after what you did to me tonight. I feigned my death in order to test you and I found you lacking Basil- lacking in every respect. You put your own selfish aspirations before mine- you were not prepared to carry out my dying wish.' 'Don't be so melodramatic Clarissa…' Basil attempted a little table turning, '…we've had quite enough of that for one night.' But Clarissa was not to be denied. 'You are trying to wriggle out of your culpability Basil, which is reprehensible. Your intention was to give me what you called a Christian burial; and very persuasive you were too in your arguments. You convinced all the others to agree to have me buried in the ground. You, Basil, were prepared to bury me in the earth and let me rot.'

'Nonsense Clarissa, I had every intention of freezing you. At first, quite naturally I was upset, taken by surprise, I was not thinking clearly, later given more time…' 'There was no time Basil…'

'I allowed Mrs. Jenkins to wrap you in aluminium foil…' 'you are a barefaced liar Basil. You told her to stop what she was doing; you said it was obscene. I heard you- I heard everything that was said and am extremely disappointing everyone's words were too.' Clarissa looked reproachfully at Charles, who, sipping the much needed whiskey, had assumed (wrongly) that he was spared. 'your behaviour was no better Hux…' 'Clarissa I was overcome- upset- distraught- I simply did not know what I was doing or saying. Of course as soon as I recovered I would have called the van…done all I could…' His fairytale petred out. 'And by then Hux, it might have been too late. I would have deteriorated, as Mrs. Jenkins so succinctly put it.' Again Basil attempted a diversion.

Chapter Twenty-Six

'Come clean Clarissa- how old are you really?' Charles knew this was not a question that would be received with equanimity; but this time Clarissa only laughed. 'You are completely impossible Basil. Oscar Wilde who knew more about women than all of you put together, said it for me-said it beautifully and precisely. "No woman should ever be quite accurate about her age- it looks so calculating." Now let's recapitulate; as far as Basil is concerned I am near sixty; for Hux I am forty-two and for Zil I am fifty odd. That is exactly as it should be and will so remain. 'I am not concerned with your age,' said Charles throwing a complacent glance at Basil, 'it does not matter to me in the least you are as beautiful as a young girl and as ageless.' Basil realised that he had lost a lot of points there but retaliated immediately. 'I may have failed your nasty little test Clarissa, but he…' Basil pointed at Charles, '…didn't show up too well ether. I asked for his advice, while you were lying dead on the floor, his advice as a so-called expert and he was useless no help at all. You heard it all Clarissa- I'm not making it up.' He had been a small boy he would at this point poked his tongue out at the outmanoeuvred Charles who, unabashed, swiftly retorted, 'At least I was genuinely upset- I'm sure you noticed that Clarissa. All he…' he pointed disparagingly at Basil, '..Thought about was his precious Hall- an instinctive and revealing reaction. Now you know what he truly thinks of you. The time has come to leave him, to leave the Hall to come away with me- please Clarissa?' Basil snorted, 'After your disappointing behaviour tonight Dr. Huxley I cannot imagine Clarissa contemplating anything utterly ridiculous.' Charles was not intimidated, he went on, 'my behaviour was certainly no worse than yours- anyway why should she stay with you- you don't love her.' 'I do- I do love her.' 'You do not- I'm the one who loves her.'

'What, Dr. Huxley has that got to do with anything? This is her home- she will not leave it.'

'She will, she is sick to death of you and of your obsession with the Hall.'

'It won't take her long to tire of you and your stupid cryonics.'

'She won't tire of me- she wants to work with me and to see the world with me.'

'What kind of life is that- living like gypsies, no stability, no roots- no she'll never agree to that.' Clarissa rose up, 'shut up both of you- SHE is tired of your squabbling- you are behaving like a couple of naughty boys. Both of you have very little to be proud of tonight.

Has it not occurred to either of you to ask me what I think? What I propose to do?' Charles and Basil cried in unison, 'what??' Subdued now Clarissa admitted, 'I'm afraid I don't know…I simply don't know.'

133

Wearily Basil slumped back into his chair. 'After all that! Another drink Dr. Huxley?' Charles tiredly slumped too.

'Why not Sir Basil,' he looked at Clarissa unhappily, 'I simply don't understand you Clarissa- I am completely baffled.' Basil poured whisky into both glasses and also addressed his wife, ''You played a filthy trick on us tonight Clarissa and if the outcome has not been to your liking then all I can say is- it serves you jolly well right.' Clarissa accepted the rebuke without retaliation. She shrugged her shoulders, 'where is the perfection we all dream of,' she said sadly, 'I must admit it was a shabby trick I played on you and I do admit that I feel a little guilty. What's more I've gained nothing. I suppose in the circumstances it does serve me right. I imagine that my childish test would be a revelation for me – I thought everything would become crystal clear in one blinding flash as it were. But now everything is as foggy as it ever was- foggier if that's possible.' All three sipped their whiskies silently- each immersed in his own thought. After a time Basil rose and picked up the telephone. He dialled and spoke, 'Basil Hare Bell here Matron- any news on my daughter-in-law? Not yet…when do you think then? It seems to be taking longer than usual this time…in another hour or so. Quite. Thank you Matron- I'll try again later.'

CHAPTER TWENTY-SEVEN

Dawn, in the multi-coloured layers of orange, grey and deep blue, streaked the sky. Clarissa rose to her feet. 'I think it's time for a cup of tea; after our all-night vigil, what else is there?' No one refuted her wisdom- the age-old panacea was to be invoked again. They trailed after her into the kitchen. Clarissa put the kettle on and searched in the larder for the pot, for the cups, for the sugar, for the tea. 'Earl Grey alright for you Basil? Hux? 'Whatever.'

Clarissa made tea, placed everything on a tray and brought it to the table. She poured. 'Milk Hux?' 'Yes please Clarissa- just a drop.' 'Basil?' 'You know how I like my tea Clarissa- why do you ask?' 'I'm tired Basil as we all are.' She handed him a cup. Before he could complain the telephone sounded. Charles took Clarissa's hand across the table, his eyes pleading with her. Basil listened earnestly, 'yes...yes... Tony... what did you say? Are you quite sure?' The receiver fell from his hand- he turned, transformed. It was as though a thousand suns had risen in his face. 'it's a boy- a 101lb boy!' he left the room as if floating on air, beaming with delight. 'Where is he going,' asked Hux, 'I don't know,' said Clarissa concerned- 'I think the news has been too much for him. I hope he doesn't have a heart attack- perhaps I'd better go and see...' At that moment Basil returned carrying a bottle of champagne and three glasses. He popped the cork and poured. 'Dom Perignon '57. I put it on ice towards the end of Teresa's every pregnancy. In the past, I have been obliged to return it to the cellar- but not tonight.' 'How incredibly sexist,' said Clarissa, 'if I'd only known what was in the cellar we would have opened a bottle every single time a baby was born. How mean of you Basil.' Basil in a euphoric haze heard nothing. 'Tonight we drink the famous drop,' he said and raised his glass, 'I propose a toast- a toast to the future of the Hare Bells- because now our future is assured. I drink to the next Basil Hare Bell...'

'And his name?' asked Charles, 'will he be called Basil Hare Bell VII or VIII?' Basil laughed merrily, 'we have no need for that sort of thing over here Dr. Huxley. What you propose is purely an American convention. Of course you people only do it to make up for your lack of tradition and very confronting even aggressive custom it is too, to saddle a poor boy which such a name. Over here that practice is reserved for Kings and Queens- no doubt that's where you Yanks got the idea.' 'I guess...' Charles gave up. He raised his glass, 'Here's congratulations Sir Basil. And good luck to the youngster.' Clarissa raised her glass too.

'Well done Basil- I'll drink to that- a toast to the latest Basil Hare Bell…' she drank, immediately screwed her faceu p and then began to laugh helplessly. 'Oh dear…my poor Basil…the champagnes gone off, you've kept it too long.' 'So it has- I didn't even notice. Have some more you two, it's not really too bad…' 'The taste of triumph must be overwhelming to mask that sourness Basil.' She continued to laugh. Charles put his glass down, and rose to his feet.' 'Oh well, it seems to me…,' he began gravely, interrupting Clarissa's laughter, '…it seems to me that I am superfluous here- I guess I'll be on my way.'

The words were like arrows, piercing Clarissa to the heart. Her breathing caught in her through. She looked first at Charles then at Basil, then again at Charles. She seemed to see him for the first time and slowly, as in a dream unfolding, the fog lifted and the view for her became crystal clear. 'Take me with you Hux- please…' dumbfounded Charles replied. 'Are you sure Clarissa…quite sure…do you mean it?' I'm sure Hux- I know it's the here and now that matters- in fact that's all there is. The future can take care of itself. Or Basil- you can take care of it.' Basil protested, 'But Clarissa- you can't leave me now- I need you more than ever.' 'On the contrary Basil- at last I see that I can leave you. The succession is assured- your life will not be empty without me.' Having waited so long for her, Charles was still finding it difficult to believe in Clarissa's assertions. 'Do you really mean to go with me Clarissa? Even as far as Australia?' Basil laughed scornfully, 'To that barbaric land- good luck to you!' Clarissa was not to be deterred. 'Even to Australia- I hear they make quite a good wine out there. And Basil you may find yourself galvanized into moneymaking action now that you have your longed- for heir. I've done my bit- injected new blood as well as new money into the Hare Bell Dynasty.' 'What do you mean by moneymaking Clarissa- what on earth could I do?'

'Think about it Basil- there are plenty of precedents amongst the aristocracy in this country- look to their example. You can open the Hall to tourists, start a zoo or a fun fair…any commercial enterprise that will make money. I may even be persuaded to help you financially with a promising scheme.' Basil considered the suggestion; ideas began to form and buzz like busy bees in his head. He nodded. He smiled. 'Come along now Hux,' Clarissa took his hand, 'Show me the world while we still have time.' Outside the sun was rising on a new day. As the birds began their insistent territorial chirping and warbling Clarissa and Charles, hand in hand, left Basil sipping bad champagne and gazing thoughtfully, even optimistically into the future.

www.ingramcontent.com/pod-product-compliance
Lightning Source LLC
Chambersburg PA
CBHW071242250626
47163CB00001B/290